The gleam in his eyes made her pulse speed up.

"You know all those times we talked on the phone?" His fingers slid down the curve of her jaw. "I didn't picture you looking quite like this."

She had to move *now,* before she did something really foolish and unprofessional—like make a pass at her client.

"I think I'll read for a while before I turn in," she said, scooting away from him. "I can't wait to read your new book, by the way. I'm really looking forward to it."

He studied her face for a moment, his gaze so intense that she wondered if he saw too much there, but then he asked, "How would you like to read it now?"

"I would love to."

He seemed amused by the fervency of her assurance. "Go on back and put your feet up, and I'll bring the manuscript to you."

"In the bedroom, you mean?"

There was an undercurrent of laughter in his voice as his eyes met hers. "That sounds good to me."

Dear Reader,

Your best bet for coping with April showers is to run—not walk—to your favorite retail outlet and check out this month's lineup. We'd like to highlight popular author Laurie Paige and her new miniseries SEVEN DEVILS. Laurie writes, "On my way to a writers' conference in Denver, I spotted the Seven Devils Mountains. This had to be checked out! Sure enough, the rugged, fascinating land proved to be ideal for a bunch of orphans who'd been demanding that their stories be told." You won't want to miss *Showdown!*, the second book in the series, which is about a barmaid and a sheriff destined for love!

Gina Wilkins dazzles us with *Conflict of Interest,* the second book in THE McCLOUDS OF MISSISSIPPI series, which deals with the combustible chemistry between a beautiful literary agent and her ruggedly handsome and reclusive author. Can they have some fun without love taking over the relationship? Don't miss Marilyn Pappano's *The Trouble with Josh,* which features a breast cancer survivor who decides to take life by storm and make the most of everything—but she never counts on sexy cowboy Josh Rawlins coming into the mix.

In Peggy Webb's *The Mona Lucy,* a meddling but well-meaning mother attempts to play Cupid to her son and a beautiful artist who is painting her portrait. Karen Rose Smith brings us *Expecting the CEO's Baby,* an adorable tale about a mix-up at the fertility clinic and a marriage of convenience between two strangers. And in Lisette Belisle's *His Pretend Wife,* an accident throws an ex-con and an ex-debutante together, making them discover that rather than enemies, they just might be soul mates!

As you can see, we have a variety of stories for our readers, which explore the essentials—life, love and family. Stay tuned next month for six more top picks from Special Edition!

Sincerely,

Karen Taylor Richman
Senior Editor

Please address questions and book requests to:
Silhouette Reader Service
U.S.: 3010 Walden Ave., P.O. Box 1325, Buffalo, NY 14269
Canadian: P.O. Box 609, Fort Erie, Ont. L2A 5X3

Conflict of
Interest

GINA WILKINS

SPECIAL EDITION™

Published by Silhouette Books

America's Publisher of Contemporary Romance

For John, who is still my strongest supporter
after all these years.

 SILHOUETTE BOOKS

ISBN 0-373-24531-9

CONFLICT OF INTEREST

This edition published by arrangement with Harlequin Books S.A.

® and ™ are trademarks of Harlequin Books S.A., used under license.
Trademarks indicated with ® are registered in the United States Patent
and Trademark Office, the Canadian Trade Marks Office and in other
countries.

Visit Silhouette at www.eHarlequin.com

Printed in U.S.A.

GINA WILKINS

is a bestselling and award-winning author who has written more than sixty-five books for Harlequin and Silhouette. She credits her successful career in romance to her long, happy marriage and her three "extraordinary" children.

A lifelong resident of central Arkansas, Ms. Wilkins sold her first book to Harlequin in 1987 and has been writing full-time ever since. She has appeared on the Waldenbooks, B. Dalton and *USA TODAY* bestseller lists. She is a three-time recipient of the Maggie Award for Excellence, sponsored by Georgia Romance Writers, and has won several awards from the reviewers of *Romantic Times*.

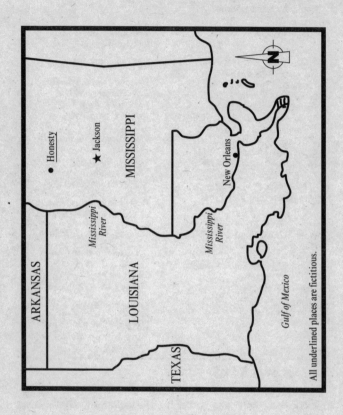

ARKANSAS

MISSISSIPPI

• Honesty

★ Jackson

Mississippi River

LOUISIANA

New Orleans

Mississippi River

TEXAS

Gulf of Mexico

All underlined places are fictitious.

Prologue

After the thirteenth unanswered ring, Adrienne Corley slammed her telephone into its cradle. She wasn't the type to lose her temper very often, but Gideon McCloud could provoke a saint into a tantrum.

It was the fifth time in the past three days that she had attempted to reach him. His answering machine had broken several weeks ago and he hadn't bothered to replace it, so she couldn't leave a message. She'd sent e-mails, but apparently he hadn't checked those in a while, either.

The worst part was that she suspected he was sitting right there beside the phone, listening to it ring and choosing not to answer.

"I do not need this aggravation," she grumbled, glaring at the phone as if her scowl would carry through the lines to the man she had been trying to reach. "I could get an easier job, you know. Working in a bank. A library, maybe. Even digging ditches would have to be better than working with eccentric, temperamental authors.''

"Threatening to quit again?'' Jacqueline Peeples, her administrative assistant, asked as she set a mountain of mail on Adrienne's desk.

"Someday I'm going through with that threat.''

"Yeah, right. Tell that to your daddy.''

Adrienne transferred her glare from the telephone to her co-worker. "I'm not afraid of my father. If I choose to quit his literary agency, I'm certainly free to do so.''

"Mmm-hmm.'' Jacqueline had heard that before, of course. She didn't believe it any more than Adrienne did. "At least you've got your vacation coming up. If I've ever seen anyone who needs two weeks away from the office, it's you. So don't you let your father try to talk you out of it again.''

"I won't,'' Adrienne vowed. "I've earned this vacation—the first I've taken in three years—and I'm going to enjoy every day of it. I'm so tired of schedules and appointments that I haven't even made any plans for the next two weeks. I'm going to act completely on impulse, take every minute as it comes.''

"That sounds like exactly what you need. But in the meantime, what are you going to do about Gideon McCloud?''

"I'm going to make him talk to me—even if I have to fly to Honesty, Mississippi, and break into his house.''

Jacqueline laughed, as Adrienne had intended. "Now *that* I would like to see.''

"Me, breaking into his house?''

"No. You in Mississippi.''

The more she thought about it, the more it seemed like a brilliant solution. Just the sort of gutsy, tough-guy move her father would make. Gideon McCloud was curt, blunt and reclusive, but he was a talented writer with a great future ahead of him, and she intended to grab a percentage of that future.

"Book me a flight," she said without giving herself a chance to think about it. "Early next week, preferably. That will give me time to get everything here cleared away."

Jacqueline's eyebrows rose. "You can't be serious. You want to go to Mississippi to meet with an author during your vacation?"

The more she thought about it, the better the idea seemed—though, of course, she *was* overworked and over-stressed. She nodded slowly, her resolve strengthening. "It'll only take a day or two, and I've never been to Mississippi, so I can count that as a vacation trip. Two birds with one stone. Let's just see if Gideon McCloud can ignore me when I'm staring directly into his eyes."

Chapter One

Gideon McCloud's telephone rang several times Monday, but he ignored it so effectively he hardly heard it. In a moment of weakness earlier that morning, he had answered a call. The unfortunate telemarketer's ears were probably still ringing from the force with which Gideon had slammed the receiver back into its cradle. He had an almost pathological aversion to telemarketers; hence, his general reluctance to answer his telephone.

He really should replace his answering machine, he mused when he became aware that the phone was ringing yet again. Maybe he would get around to that sometime later in the week. Then he focused on his computer screen and tuned everything else out.

Perhaps another half hour passed before he was distracted from work by his doorbell. It chimed half a dozen times, followed by a pounding on the door, followed by someone leaning on the doorbell again.

Muttering beneath his breath, he shoved himself away from the keyboard and stalked through his immaculate house to the front door, which he jerked open impatiently. *"What?"*

A tall, slender woman in her early sixties stood on his doorstep, holding the hand of a blond cherub with shoulder-length curls and huge blue eyes. A large, wheeled, red suitcase rested on the porch between them, and the little girl carried a bulging purple backpack. Gideon frowned at the luggage for a moment before slowly lifting his gaze to his mother's face. "What's going on?"

"If you would pick up your telephone, you would already know the answer to that." Without waiting for an invitation, Lenore McCloud stepped past him into his entryway, dragging the suitcase with one hand and holding the little girl's hand in her other.

Gideon closed the door behind them, then turned to face his mother. He was still unnerved by the sight of that suitcase. "Well?"

"Your aunt Wanda fell during the night and broke her hip. It was several hours before anyone found her, and she's in bad shape now. Her neighbor called me a couple of hours ago, and I need to go there immediately."

Because his aunt was the only surviving member of his mother's immediate family, Gideon wasn't surprised she felt the need to rush to Wanda's side. "I'm sorry to hear that. I hope she'll be okay."

"Yes, so do I." Lenore glanced down at the still-silent little girl. "Isabelle, sweetie, the den is right through that door. Why don't you run in there and watch cartoons for a few minutes while I talk with Gideon?"

The child nodded obediently and disappeared into the den. A moment later Gideon heard the opening strains of "Scooby-dooby-doo…"

''Why is she watching cartoons in my den?'' he asked his mother suspiciously.

''Isabelle's going to stay with you until I can make other arrangements. I hope it will only be for a few days, but I can't make any guarantees.''

Shaking his head, Gideon had both hands in the air before she even finished speaking. ''No way, Mom. Forget it. You can't leave her here.''

Lenore wore the stern, don't-mess-with-me expression he remembered very well from his youth. ''There really is no other choice. Nathan and Caitlin won't be back from their honeymoon for nearly two weeks. Deborah went back to Florida yesterday. And I can hardly take a four-year-old with me to the hospital.''

''What about the housekeeper who watches Isabelle while Nathan's working? Can't she stay with her?''

''Mrs. Tuckerman left right after the wedding Saturday for a two-week cruise with her bridge club. It seemed like a good idea for her vacation to coincide with Nathan's honeymoon, especially since I had volunteered to watch Isabelle. No one could have predicted Wanda's accident, of course.''

Gideon could feel the cage bars closing around him, but he tried one last time to escape. ''Surely there's someone else. I have to work, and you know how I get when I'm past deadline. Leaving a four-year-old with me probably constitutes reckless endangerment of a minor or something.''

''Don't be ridiculous. You're perfectly capable of watching Isabelle for a few days. She's a very well-behaved child, no trouble at all. She's in preschool from eight in the morning until two in the afternoon, so you can work in your usual solitude during those hours.''

"And after two? What am I supposed to do with her then?"

"You're an intelligent young man. You'll manage."

"I don't *want* to manage. You can't leave her here."

"Fine." Lenore gave him a wounded look. "Since I have no other options, I'll take Isabelle back to my house. I'll call my poor sister and tell her I can't come to her when she needs me because it isn't convenient for my son."

He groaned. "Mother—"

She held up a hand. "It's all right. I understand. You're an important writer, and your time is very valuable."

The cage doors slammed shut. Gideon was trapped, and he knew it. He sighed. "Go to your sister. I'll watch the kid."

If Lenore had harbored any doubt that he would eventually capitulate, it didn't show in her expression. She pulled a folded sheet of paper from the leather purse dangling from her arm. "This is the schedule Nathan and Caitlin left for me with Isabelle's preschool and dance class times."

"Dance class?"

Ignoring his groan, she continued, "You also have the phone numbers for her school and her pediatrician, and a number where Nathan can be reached in an emergency. I've written a couple of numbers for myself at the bottom of the page, and you have my cell number, of course."

"How long do you expect to be gone?"

"I'm not sure. I'll let you know as soon as I can. Isabelle had lunch at school today, of course, and I gave her a snack after I picked her up. She'll probably be hungry for dinner around six, and she should be in bed by eight. Try to make sure she eats healthily. Don't let her have too many snacks or junk foods. Now I really must be on my way, since I have a two-hour drive ahead of me. I'll just step in to say goodbye to Isabelle.''

His footsteps dragging, Gideon followed Lenore into his den. Isabelle sat curled on one corner of his suede-leather sofa, the cartoon she had selected playing on the television across the room. She looked away from the screen when they entered, her expression uncertain. ''I'm staying here?''

''For a few days,'' Lenore agreed, giving the child a bracing smile. ''You'll be fine, sweetie. Your big brother will take very good care of you.''

Because he wasn't used to thinking of himself as Isabelle's big brother—after all, he'd met the child for the first time less than four months ago—it took him a beat to realize that his mother expected him to say something then. ''You're welcome to stay here, Isabelle.''

He didn't blame her for looking less than enthusiastic. She was probably well aware that he was completely ill-equipped to care for a small child. Though he knew she was gregarious and talkative with other people—even total strangers—she had been rather reserved with him during the few occasions they'd been together. She had treated him with a somewhat wary shyness that had told him she didn't quite know what to make of him, and since he'd never decided quite what he felt about her, he'd been content to leave things just that way between them. Distantly civil.

He'd certainly never expected to find himself baby-sitting her.

''I have to go, sweetie. Be good for Gideon, okay? And be patient with him,'' Lenore said a bit wryly. ''Sometimes he's a slow learner. But he'll be very nice to you,'' she added, giving her son a meaningful look.

Isabelle wrapped her arms around Lenore's neck. "Goodbye, Nanna. I hope your sister gets all better soon."

Gideon still found it strange to hear his half sister refer to his mother by that grandmotherly nickname. It hadn't been very long ago when Lenore hadn't even wanted to acknowledge the child's existence. Now here she was taking full responsibility for her ex-husband's kid while her oldest son, the orphaned child's legal guardian, was away on his honeymoon, and hugging her as affectionately as if she really were Isabelle's grandmother.

It was no wonder, Gideon mused with a shake of his head, that most people in this town tended to think of Lenore, a tireless, generous community volunteer, as a near saint. They had no such illusions about *him*, however.

Ten minutes later he found himself alone with a four-year-old who gazed up at him expectantly, waiting for him to say or do something. He didn't have a clue where to begin.

He glanced at his watch. It wasn't even 4:00 p.m. yet. Too early for dinner. Four hours away from her bedtime. "So, uh, do you want a drink or something?" he asked awkwardly. "I have some soda, I think. And fruit juice."

She shook her head. "No, thank you."

"Oh. Well." He looked around the room, which was decorated in Southwestern style with leather, distressed woods, pottery, western paintings and Remington bronzes. The walls were lined with shelves almost filled to overflowing with hardcover and paperback books. It was a guy's room, and there was nothing in it to entertain a child except the television she had been watching.

"I need to finish something in my office," he said. "Will you be okay in here watching TV?"

She nodded gravely. "I'll be okay."

She looked awfully tiny sitting there on his big couch. "If you need anything, just let me know, okay?"

"Okay."

He practically bolted out of the room. His office had always been a retreat for him, but it seemed even more a refuge now. Unfortunately, he knew he couldn't stay locked in there until his mother returned to free him.

Gideon had been sitting in front of his computer for half an hour when a sound from the doorway pulled his concentration away from the computer screen. To his frustration he'd managed to type maybe two sentences since he'd sat down, so he was frowning when he looked up.

Annoyance turned to consternation when he spotted Isabelle standing just inside the doorway, a stuffed white owl cuddled against her chest and a pitiful quiver in her lower lip. She looked to be on the verge of tears, which was enough to make Gideon panic.

"What's wrong?" he asked, pushing away from the computer. "Did you hurt yourself?"

She shook her head. "I heard a noise outside the window. It scared me."

Exhaling slowly in relief, he shoved a hand through his already disheveled dark hair. A brisk, mid-March wind was blowing outside, and he suspected she'd heard a tree branch tapping against the house. "There's nothing scary outside, Isabelle," he assured her. "Just a couple of trees planted next to the den windows. It isn't even dark out yet."

A fat tear rolled slowly down her cheek. "It's lonely in the den."

He supposed it was natural for her to be upset. The child had been through a great deal of trauma in the past year. She'd lost her parents in an accident, had been uprooted from her home in California and resettled in her oldest half brother's home here in Mississippi and was now with a half brother she hardly knew. A brother who had no idea how to comfort an upset child.

"Can I stay in here with you?" Isabelle asked. "I promise I'll be quiet."

He glanced toward the writing desk he used for paying bills. "You can sit at this desk. Do you like to draw pictures?"

She nodded, her expression brightening.

"I've got the only refrigerator in town with no artwork stuck on the front with magnets. Maybe you can draw something for my fridge."

She seemed to like that idea.

He dug out a stack of printer paper, several pencils and a box of colored markers from his supply closet and piled them on the desk after moving a teetering tower of unopened mail out of the way. He had no toys in the house, but plenty of art provisions, since he was seriously addicted to office supply stores. Isabelle settled into the big chair behind the writing desk, and Gideon returned to his computer.

True to her word, Isabelle was very quiet as she contentedly scribbled and colored, but Gideon still found himself unable to concentrate on his writing. He wasn't accustomed to having anyone else in his house when he worked, much less in the same room with him. After writing and deleting the same sentence for the fourth time, he muttered a curse beneath his breath and punched a key to close the file.

"What's the matter, Gideon?"

She had a unique way of pronouncing his name, he mused. Nothing he could pinpoint, exactly, but it sounded different when she said it. "Nothing's wrong," he lied.

"Are you writing another book?"

"Trying to."

"Nate said you write good books, but they're not for kids."

She always shortened Nathan's name so casually, but then, Isabelle had known Nathan all her life. He had been the only one of the three elder McCloud siblings to maintain a relationship with their father after the bitter divorce from their mother a few months before Isabelle's birth. "No, I don't write children's books."

"What are your books about?"

"Most people call them thrillers. They have elements of science fiction and fantasy in them and what has been referred to as dark humor."

She blinked a couple of times in response to his dry description, then said, "I like Dr. Seuss."

Her matter-of-fact statement made Gideon grin. "So do I."

His smile seemed to take her by surprise. She studied his face a moment, then smiled back at him before returning her attention to her artwork.

Okay, Gideon thought. Maybe this wouldn't be so tough after all. How hard could it be to keep an eye on an exceptionally bright and well-behaved four-year-old?

It was cloudy and dark by 7:00 p.m. on that Monday evening, and a cold drizzle had begun to fall, blown in on a strong northern front. Not a very experienced driver in the first place, since she rarely needed a car in the city, Adrienne struggled a bit with the unfamiliar rental car on the bumpy Mississippi road. She'd gotten lost twice before she found the town of Honesty, then had some difficulty finding anyone to give her directions to Gideon's address.

She should have known, she thought as she carefully

negotiated a winding gravel road, that Gideon would live well outside of town. She was definitely forming a mental picture of a crusty hermit who was more comfortable with the characters in his head than the people in the real world.

She had never met him—had never even seen a photograph of him—but she'd talked to him several times on the telephone during the past two years since he had signed with her father's literary agency. Mostly, their communication had been through letters and faxes. She loved his books, but she hadn't been able to get to know him very well through their limited contact.

Based strictly on his behavior, she had formed a mental image of him that wasn't particularly flattering. She guessed that he was in his late thirties or early forties. A bit geeky, most likely. Probably a real oddball. He wouldn't be the first talented writer she had met who was downright strange.

He *was* the first she'd bothered to track down this way— something she couldn't explain. She had decided her motives were a combination of wanting to impress her father with her professional cleverness and the fact that she absolutely loved Gideon McCloud's books.

His house looked normal enough—a neat frame bungalow tucked into a woody hillside. The lot was naturally landscaped with mulch and ground cover, which would require a minimum of effort to keep it looking nice. And it did look nice, she had to admit. She'd bet it was really pretty later in the spring, when the trees and bushes would be in full bloom, and in the fall when the surrounding hillsides would be ablaze with color.

Okay, so she liked his home. And more than liked his writing. That certainly didn't mean she would like *him*.

Parking at the end of the long gravel driveway, she climbed out of the rental car. As she hunched into her clothing against the chilly mist, she wished she'd brought a heavier coat. The wind seemed to slice right through the leather jacket she wore over a black pantsuit.

There was only one pole lamp on the property, and as far as Adrienne was concerned, it cast more spooky shadows than it eliminated. Moving swiftly but carefully over the slick rock walkway that led to the porch steps, she could almost feel the eyes of hungry night creatures following her progress. It was so quiet she was sure she could hear her own heart pounding. Who could sleep out here without the soothing sounds of cab horns and emergency sirens, muffled shouts and the clatter of garbage trucks?

She was relieved to duck under his covered porch, out of the mist. Tossing her damp auburn hair out of her face, she paused for a few moments to catch her breath before reaching for the doorbell. There were lights burning in the windows and sounds coming from inside, so she knew someone was home. Showing up unannounced on his doorstep was hardly proper business etiquette, but it wasn't as if she could have called and let him know she was on her way. He wouldn't have answered the phone if she'd tried.

She had to ring the bell a second time before the door finally opened. Her first thought was that this could not possibly be Gideon McCloud. This man was young—no older than thirty—and incredibly good-looking, with tousled dark hair, long-lashed green eyes and an athlete's body clad in a gray sweatshirt, washed-soft jeans and running shoes. Maybe she had the wrong house.

But then he spoke—or rather, barked at her—and she knew she had the right man, after all. "What do you want?"

"Are you Gideon McCloud?" she asked, more a formality than an inquiry.

"Yes. Who are you?" His tone was impatient, his attention obviously focused elsewhere.

"I'm Adrienne Corley. Your agent," she added, in case the name didn't immediately register.

At least that got his attention. "What the hell are you doing here?"

Before she could answer, a child's wail sounded from behind them. "Gideon! I still can't find Hedwig."

Gideon grimaced, then held the door wider. "Come in. You can help us look for—"

"Gideon!"

He shoved a hand through his hair, explaining its disarray. "I'm coming, Isabelle."

Closing the door behind Adrienne, he turned and walked away, motioning for her to follow. Thoroughly confused, she trailed after him, her bulging briefcase tucked beneath her arm.

She noted in a quick, sweeping glance that the room they entered was a neatly furnished, Southwestern-style den. In the center of the room, dressed in a white nightgown with pink ribbons, stood a little girl with the angelically beautiful face of a Sandra Kuck cherub. Framed in a cloud of golden curls, her rosy cheeks were tear-streaked, her huge blue eyes flooded. Even as Adrienne watched, another teardrop escaped to slide slowly down her face.

"Your daughter?" she asked Gideon.

"My sister," he answered curtly. "Isabelle."

Sister? The child couldn't be more than four.

"Gideon?" The little girl's lower lip quivered as she spoke. "I've looked *everywhere*."

"Then we'll have to look again," he said. "My house isn't that big, and you've only been here a few hours. Your toy couldn't have simply disappeared."

He turned toward the doorway. "I'll go look in the office and the kitchen again. You two keep searching in here.''

"Um, what are we looking *for?*" Adrienne called after him.

"Hedwig," Isabelle replied.

"A stuffed toy owl," Gideon clarified over his shoulder. "White."

Left alone with the woebegone child, Adrienne looked uncertainly around the room. "Where have you looked?"

"Everywhere."

Adrienne drew a deep breath and moved toward the suede couch. She laid her briefcase and leather jacket at one end, then turned toward the child. "Okay, let's look again."

They searched behind the cushions and beneath the couch, then peered under a big leather recliner and a couple of armchairs covered in a Southwestern tapestry fabric. Their efforts netted nothing. There weren't even any dust bunnies beneath the furniture. She wished Gideon's housekeeper lived in New York; Adrienne could use someone this scrupulous, she thought, recalling her own string of less-than-dedicated domestic workers.

Sitting back on her heels, she looked at Isabelle again. The child had been peering under tables and behind the television cabinet to no avail. Adrienne could hear doors opening and closing forcefully in another part of the house, probably the kitchen, the slams accompanied by a low mutter that was very likely a string of unintelligible curses. Gideon wasn't having any better luck with his own search, obviously.

Remembering what he'd said, Adrienne spoke to Isabelle. "You've only been here a few hours?"

The child nodded. "Nanna brought me."

"And you haven't been anywhere else since?"

Isabelle shook her head. "I've been right here."

"You had your owl when you got here?"

Another nod.

"Okay." Adrienne stood. "Tell me everything you've done since you arrived."

Isabelle puckered her face in thought. "I watched TV, and I drew pictures in Gideon's office."

"He said he would look in the office."

The child sniffed. "He already did. He looked all over it."

"What did you do after you drew pictures?"

"I had dinner. Gideon made spaghetti. I spilled some on my clothes," she added, her lip quivering again, "so Gideon told me to change into my pajamas."

"You changed in a bedroom?"

"No. In the bathroom, because I had to wash spaghetti off my face and hands."

"Where did you put the clothes you had on before?"

"In the hamper."

Adrienne held out her hand. "Show me."

Slipping her little fingers into Adrienne's, Isabelle led her down a short hallway to a small bathroom papered in a muted plaid and fitted with oak cabinets and a marble sink and tub. White globe lights framed the beveled mirror over the sink, and a wicker hamper stood beneath a print of ducks in flight at sunrise.

Isabelle opened the hinged lid of the hamper and pointed at the brightly colored knits tumbled in the bottom. "Those are mine."

Adrienne reached in to pick up the spaghetti-sauce-splashed shirt and slacks. Two brown plastic eyes stared up at her from the bottom of the hamper. "Is this a friend of yours?" she asked with a faint smile, holding the toy up for Isabelle's inspection.

The child's face brightened with a broad, dimpled smile. "Hedwig!"

Adrienne watched as Isabelle hugged the stuffed owl tightly, and then she said, "We'd better go tell your brother we found it."

"He'll be glad. I think he was getting sort of mad. It's hard to tell with Gideon, though."

Adrienne couldn't help chuckling. "Is it?"

"Mmm-hmm." As naturally as if they'd known each other for a long time, she reached up to take Adrienne's hand again as they moved into the hallway. "I don't think Gideon's used to being around kids."

Adrienne was intrigued by Isabelle's mannerisms. She was such a tiny little thing, yet her self-possession seemed years ahead of her age. Adrienne suspected she'd spent a great deal of time with adults. "You don't *think* he's used to kids? Don't you know?"

"I haven't known him very long," Isabelle confided, then pulled Adrienne into an airy kitchen, where Gideon was peering into an oven.

The little girl seemed to find the sight amusing. "Hedwig's not in the oven, Gideon. He's right here."

Closing the oven door, Gideon turned to stare at the child who had transformed from tearful to cheery. "Where was it?"

"We found him in the clothes hamper. She, um, what's your name?" Isabelle suddenly thought to ask Adrienne.

"I'm Adrienne Corley."

Isabelle nodded gravely and turned back to Gideon. "Miss Corley found him."

Gideon released a pent-up breath. "Good. Now why don't you and Hagar go watch TV or something while Ms. Corley and I talk a few minutes?"

"It's not Hagar, it's Hedwig," Adrienne corrected him before Isabelle could do so. "From Harry Potter, right?"

Isabelle smiled and nodded, then skipped out of the room with her owl. Adrienne watched her leave, then turned to find Gideon looking at her questioningly.

"I'm in publishing," she informed him. "I know about Harry Potter."

"You want some coffee or something? I could use some myself. Actually, a couple of shots of bourbon sound pretty good right now, but since I'm baby-sitting, I guess I'd better stick with coffee."

"Coffee sounds good. Thanks."

He waved her to one of the four chairs grouped around a round oak pedestal table. "Have a seat. Want something to eat? I've got some lemon pound cake I bought at the bakery yesterday."

"That sounds great," she said, realizing only then how hungry she was. She'd missed dinner during her travel adventures.

A few minutes later she found herself sitting across the table from Gideon, cake and coffee in front of them. It was somewhat disconcerting to be facing him that way, after the unexpected chaos surrounding her arrival. The search for Hedwig had certainly been an ice-breaker, but now she was having a bit of trouble getting her mind back to business.

She couldn't stop thinking about how attractive he was, with those amazing green eyes and that brooding mouth, and his thick, dark hair. She noted only as an objective observer, she assured herself—someone who had reason to imagine his photograph on the back of a book jacket.

As for anything more than that, she still wasn't even sure she liked the guy.

Chapter Two

Gideon studied the woman sitting across his kitchen table. She didn't look exactly the way he'd pictured her during their telephone conversations. She was younger, for one thing, no older than his own thirty years, if that. And prettier, with glossy auburn hair and dark-chocolate eyes set in a creamy heart-shaped face. Nice figure, too, the type he referred to as "society sleek." Small bust, narrow waist, slender hips, long legs—all nicely toned.

Definitely a big-city girl, as out of place here in rural Mississippi as he would have been in the juice bar of her trendy health club. "So why are you here? We didn't have an appointment or anything, did we?"

Apparently savoring every bite of her cake, she shook her head. "I've been unable to reach you to set up an appointment. And I *have* tried," she added, a touch of accusation in her tone.

He shrugged without apology. "I haven't had a chance to check the mail in a while."

"Or e-mail, apparently. And you don't have an answering machine. I sent two registered letters—both of which you signed for—but you never replied. I didn't know what else to do except come here myself."

He supposed maybe he should express a little regret at her inconvenience. "Sorry. I tend to ignore the rest of the world when I near the end of a book. I've been told it's not a particularly admirable trait."

"So you *are* nearing the end of the book?"

"Is that why you're here?" he asked instead of answering. "To find out how the book's going?"

"That's one of the reasons. Since your deadline was three weeks ago and I haven't heard from you, I thought there might be a problem. I have some other business to discuss with you, also. Since I wasn't able to give you advance notice of my arrival, I certainly understand if this is an inconvenient time for you. I would be glad to make an appointment with you for a later date—either a telephone conference or another face-to-face meeting."

"What sort of business do you want to discuss?"

"The offers on your next book, for one thing. And the promotional opportunities for the one you're working on now. Your publisher wants to give this one a big marketing push—book tours, national TV, print interviews, that sort of thing. I have several pages of paperwork I want you to look over."

He winced. The very thought of a book tour gave him a headache. Having to deal with all those people? It was enough to make any respectable recluse shudder. "I really can't discuss this tonight. It's been a stressful afternoon, to say the least, and frankly, I'm too tired to think about promotion. Besides, I've got to get Isabelle bunked down for the night."

She nodded, her expression resigned. "Tomorrow, perhaps?"

"Maybe," he said, though he couldn't imagine he'd be any more in the mood then. As she had pointed out, he was already past deadline on the current book, and he wanted nothing more than to be left alone to work on it. It seemed as though everyone was conspiring to keep him from doing so.

Adrienne nodded. "If you'll direct me to the nearest hotel, I'll call you tomorrow about a convenient time to meet."

He chuckled dryly. "Closest we have to a hotel within an hour's drive are a couple of bargain-rate motels out on the main highway."

Her jaw seemed to tighten a bit, but she said only, "I'm sure that will be fine."

"Tell you what," he said on an impulse. "Why don't you stay here tonight? Isabelle has the spare bedroom, but you can take my bed. I'll sleep on the couch in the office."

"Oh, no, I—"

He silenced her with a quick slice of his hand. "If you're worried about inconveniencing me, don't. I sleep in there half the time, anyway."

Actually, the more he thought about it, the more it seemed like a good idea. Since Isabelle was staying overnight, and since she had responded well to Adrienne, maybe Adrienne could help him keep an eye on the kid during the night. Maybe even help her get ready for school in the morning; after all, what did he know about dressing a little girl, fixing her hair, that sort of thing? Since he seemed to be stuck with them for the night, he might as well make the best of the situation.

And very soon, he hoped, he would have his house to himself again. Just the way he liked it.

As Adrienne lay in bed that night—Gideon McCloud's bed, she reminded herself, shifting restlessly on the crisp, clean sheets she had put on herself—she wondered if she had made a monumental mistake when she'd rather impulsively left New York. She certainly hadn't expected to find herself staying overnight with him and his little sister.

She wondered what the story was with little Isabelle. She doubted they were full siblings, with a twenty-six-year gap between them. Had Gideon's father, like her own, chosen a young trophy bride for his second marriage? At least Adrienne was spared the embarrassment of late-life half siblings. Lawrence Corley hadn't particularly wanted *her,* much less any more offspring at this stage of his life.

She really should have insisted on finding another place to stay for the night, even if she had to make use of one of those bargain-rate motels Gideon had mentioned. She wasn't sure why she hadn't put up more of an argument. She'd found herself agreeing almost before she'd realized what she was doing.

What was it about him she found so persuasive? Sure, he was handsome, but she was accustomed to being around striking men. His green eyes were uncomfortably perceptive but hardly hypnotic. She'd been aware of a tug of attraction, but she had never allowed her hormones to guide her actions before.

So what was she doing in his bed?

She and Gideon hadn't engaged in much conversation after she had agreed to stay the night. Somehow she'd found herself tucking Isabelle into bed and reading her a bedtime story—a suggestion that had come from Gideon. By the time Isabelle was asleep, Gideon had been closed into his office and settled at his computer. He'd looked up from his work only long enough to absently inform Adrienne where she could find the clean linens. As an afterthought he had added that she should let him know if she needed anything, but she suspected he was hoping there would be no further interruptions.

She had spent the rest of the evening reading one of the manuscripts she'd brought with her. After watching the local ten-o'clock news, she'd turned in a good two hours earlier than she would have usually gone to bed. Gideon had not once emerged from his office.

Rolling onto her side, she closed her eyes, but sleep proved elusive. It was much too quiet. She could hear every gust of wind, not to mention hooting owls and the occasional moo from a distant cow. As soon as she had Gideon's signature on several contracts, she was heading back to civilization and her long-overdue vacation.

Groggy and disoriented, Adrienne woke after a restless night when the morning sun hit her full in the face. Either Gideon was an early riser, she thought, glaring at the sheer curtains that allowed the dawning sun into the room, or he was a heavy sleeper who wasn't bothered by the light.

The bedside clock read six-forty-five when she climbed out of bed and moved into the adjoining bath. By seven-fifteen, she had showered, dried her hair and dressed in one of the two casual outfits she had packed with the two professional pantsuits she'd brought with her. Smoothing her thin, emerald-green sweater over comfortably tailored black slacks, she left Gideon's bedroom.

Gideon and Isabelle were in the kitchen, and from the look of things, the morning was not running smoothly. Isabelle's fine blond hair was a pillow-tangled mess, and there was a smear of grape jelly on her chin. She wore a

long-sleeved pink T-shirt festooned with cartoon characters Adrienne didn't recognize and black leggings that
ended just above her bare feet. A half-eaten bowl of cereal
sat in front of her, along with the remains of two jelly-
spread slices of wheat toast and a half glass of milk.

Dressed in a wrinkled T-shirt and jeans, Gideon stood
nearby, his dark hair in its apparently usual disarray, a look
of impatience on his unshaven face. Just as Adrienne entered the room, he glanced at the microwave clock and
said, "Isabelle, if you don't hurry with your breakfast,
you're going to be late for school. How can anyone take
this long to eat a bowl of cereal?"

"I was reading the cereal box," the child explained. "It
has funny jokes on the back."

"You can already read?" Adrienne asked as she walked
straight to the coffeemaker on the counter next to Gideon.

"I can read the easy words," Isabelle answered, her
tone somewhere between modest and boastful.

"And you're only four?"

"Just turned four," Gideon said. "The kid is smart, but
she's *very* slow," he added with a meaningful look at Isabelle's cereal bowl.

Isabelle dutifully spooned another bite into her mouth.
Adrienne accepted the coffee mug Gideon offered her and
filled it with strong, fragrant black coffee. She sipped the
brew gratefully, feeling the jolt of caffeine clear her mind.
"When does Isabelle's school start?"

"Eight," Gideon muttered with another impatient
glance at his watch.

"I suppose we'd better hurry, then." She set her mug
down and moved toward the table. "Isabelle, it's time to
finish getting ready. Let's go do your hair, brush your teeth
and find your shoes."

"She hasn't finished her cereal," Gideon pointed out.

Adrienne shrugged. "She won't starve. My father sent me to school plenty of times with my breakfast half-eaten because I'd dawdled. I learned to eat in a timely fashion or be hungry before lunchtime."

Gideon gave it a moment's thought, then nodded. "Makes sense. Go with Adrienne, Isabelle. Tomorrow morning you'll have to save your cereal-box reading until you're completely ready for school."

Though her lower lip protruded just a bit, Isabelle slipped out of her chair and followed Adrienne out of the kitchen.

With Adrienne supervising, it took less than ten minutes to get Isabelle groomed and shod. "She's still going to be late," Gideon predicted, retrieving his car keys from a drawer in a table near the front door. "But at least it'll only be by a few minutes. Why don't you come with us, and I'll buy you breakfast after we drop Isabelle off?"

Business breakfasts and lunches were commonplace for her, so she nodded. "Sounds good. But breakfast is on me. I'm the one putting you out."

"We'll argue about the check later. Let's go."

Because Gideon drove a pickup, they decided to strap Isabelle's booster seat in the back of Adrienne's rental car to give them more room. Adrienne gave him the keys and slid into the passenger seat. She waited in the car while he escorted Isabelle into Miss Thelma's Preschool. He wasn't gone long, and he was scowling when he returned.

"Miss Thelma dressed me down for bringing Isabelle late," he muttered. "Talked to me like I was one of her preschoolers."

Adrienne winced. "How did you respond?"

"I told her I was doing the best I could under the circumstances, and if she didn't like it, too bad. Prissy old biddy."

"I hope you didn't add that last part aloud."

"No. Not this time, anyway."

"Admirable restraint."

"I thought so."

"Isabelle's parents are away, I take it?"

"Isabelle's parents—my father and his second wife—are dead," Gideon replied with a bluntness that startled her. "They died in an accident last year. Isabelle lives with my older brother, Nathan, who's away on his honeymoon. He was married Saturday morning."

"So you're baby-sitting."

"I wasn't supposed to be. My mother volunteered for that task, but she had to leave town yesterday because of a medical emergency with her sister. She didn't have anywhere else to leave the kid, so she dumped Isabelle with me."

Adrienne frowned a bit as she tried to understand his family tree. "Your mother was baby-sitting Isabelle?"

"Yes. Ironically enough, she's become a sort of surrogate grandmother to the child my father created with someone else while my mother was still married to him."

Before Adrienne could come up with a suitable response—if there was one—he turned the car into the parking lot of a metal-sided diner that looked as though it had been built in the 1950s. Most of the clientele appeared to drive pickup trucks. She noticed when Gideon escorted her inside that male customers outnumbered the women, and the majority of both genders wore blue-collar working clothes. The clatter of dishes and flatware melded with conversation and laughter to create a welcoming din.

The blue-jeaned, T-shirted, early-thirties redhead working the cash register just inside the door greeted Gideon with an eager smile that dimmed a few watts when she spotted Adrienne. "Just find yourselves a table," she said to Gideon. "Carla will be with you in a minute."

Adrienne couldn't help noticing that Gideon barely gave the woman a second glance as he nodded and led the way into the busy diner. Signs dangling from the ceiling designated the smoking and nonsmoking sections, but since it was only one big room with no dividers, it seemed to Adrienne to be a rather meaningless gesture. Gideon chose a booth at the back of the nonsmoking area, where the haze seemed a bit thinner. Accustomed to restaurants that did not allow smoking at all, Adrienne blinked a bit to clear her burning eyes, her nose twitching against the acrid odor.

"Guess I should have asked if you suffer from allergies or anything," Gideon commented belatedly. "There are still a lot of folks around here who haven't kicked the habit."

"I suppose I can tolerate the secondhand smoke for the duration of a meal."

He plucked a plastic-coated menu from a stand that also held salt, pepper, ketchup and hot sauce. "Trust me, the food here is worth the discomfort," he said as he handed her the menu.

Glancing down at the breakfast list, she mentally winced at the calorie counts of some of the features. Fried eggs, fried sausage, fried bacon, fried hash browns, buttered grits and biscuits with sausage gravy. Heart attack on a plate.

A heavyset woman with teased gray hair and a pleasantly lined face set a steaming mug of coffee in front of Gideon, then offered a second mug to Adrienne. "I already know what Gideon wants," she drawled. "What can I get you, hon?"

Adrienne ordered one scrambled egg, an order of dry toast and a fruit cup.

"Are you sure that's all you want?" Gideon asked.

"The omelets and hot cakes are both great here, and nobody makes better biscuits."

"He's right about that," their server said ruefully. "Take it from someone who's eaten way too many of them."

Adrienne thought of the lemon pound cake she'd eaten in lieu of dinner the night before. "I'd better stick with my original order," she said with a touch of regret.

Their waitress nodded and moved away.

"Are you always so disciplined?" Gideon asked.

"Not always. But I try."

He grunted and sipped his coffee, apparently considering the subject of breakfast food closed. Adrienne noticed that they were receiving quite a bit of attention from other diners, both covertly and openly. Gideon was obviously a frequent customer here, but there seemed to be a lot of speculative interest in her. The only greetings Gideon had exchanged with the other diners were a few cordial nods. She wondered if the others kept their distance because of her presence or if Gideon generally discouraged small talk.

For some reason, she suspected it was primarily the latter.

The waitress returned in an amazingly short time with their food. "Is this one of your writer friends, Gideon?" she asked casually as she served them.

"My agent," he replied, reaching for the salt shaker. "Adrienne Corley, meet Carla Booker."

"It's nice to meet you, Ms. Booker."

The older woman chuckled. "You just call me Carla, hon. Everyone does. Are you from up north?"

"New York."

"Well, isn't that something?"

"I think Joe Huebner is trying to get your attention over

there," Gideon said. "Probably wants to start on his second pot of coffee."

Carla grinned. "You're probably right. Nice to meet you, Miz Corley. Y'all give a holler if you need anything else."

The platter in front of Gideon was completely filled with a huge omelet oozing with cheese, ham, onions, peppers and mushrooms, a side order of buttered grits and two fat, fluffy-looking biscuits with a bowl of cream gravy. She watched as he dumped salsa on the omelet. "Are you always this *un*disciplined?"

"When I eat breakfast at home, I usually have cereal or a bagel. But when I eat here, I have what I want."

Had to be a guy thing, she thought with a slight sigh. She was probably gaining weight just looking at his breakfast. Gideon, on the other hand, was shoveling it in with almost sensual pleasure, and there wasn't a superfluous ounce anywhere on his extremely fine body.

She speared a chunk of cantaloupe from a bowl of mixed melons and strawberries. "Are you ready to discuss business?"

"Not while I'm eating." He scooped a bite of grits into his mouth.

Gideon McCloud was definitely a difficult client, even among the group of often demanding, sometimes neurotic and frequently temperamental writers she dealt with on a daily basis. The others were usually eager to hear exciting offers, to grab every chance to advance their careers and increase their recognition. Gideon seemed to want to write in complete anonymity.

Though he had turned down a few early offers he didn't consider rewarding enough, he didn't seem to be motivated solely by money, since he'd also shown little interest in several very lucrative propositions. He had approved the release of very little biographical material, had not provided photographs for publicity purposes—even though he certainly had the right look—and had expressed absolutely no enthusiasm for book tours or interviews or even a promotional Web site.

Because she sensed that he was on the verge of a breakthrough with his writing, his lack of cooperation frustrated Adrienne. Her father was becoming impatient with her inability to get Gideon to commit to the newest offers, and he had been hinting that he might have to take this client in hand himself.

But she sensed that she would get nowhere by pushing Gideon before he was ready. She concentrated on her breakfast and directed the conversation away from his work. "We seem to be attracting attention. I suppose your acquaintances are wondering who I am."

He glanced around briefly—causing several heads to turn abruptly away—and then returned to his food. "They all know who you are by now. Carla's told them you're my agent from New York. Now they're wondering why you're here. She'll be back in a bit to try to find out for them."

"Word travels fast here."

"You have no idea."

She watched the other diners with discreet curiosity during the remainder of the meal, intrigued by the contrasts between big-city and small-town dynamics. Here, everyone seemed to know everyone else, and even those who appeared to be strangers tended to exchange "good mornings," even to strike up conversations as they stood in line to pay at the old-fashioned cash register.

She saw quite a few wide hips encased in stretch fabrics, teased hair in questionable shades of blond, beer bellies sagging over drooping blue jeans, farm equipment caps and camouflage—stereotypes she had expected to find in rural Mississippi. But the rumble of laughter and low drawls of conversation, mingled with the smell of coffee and food, proved to be pleasantly relaxing. Adrienne found herself enjoying the simple meal quite a bit, even without much conversation from her taciturn companion.

Carla stopped by the table with a coffee carafe. "Y'all doing okay?"

Adrienne held out her mug. "Fine, thank you. The food is very good."

"Well, thank you. Are you here on business with Gideon, Miz Corley?"

"Yes, I am."

The woman nodded her tightly teased gray head. "I thought you must be. Bet you got some movie or TV offers for him, hmm? I said when I read that last book of his that it would sure make a good movie. I think you need to hire Mel Gibson and Julia Roberts to be in it. Don't get any of those flash-in-the-pan teenyboppers who show off their belly buttons more than their talent. That would just ruin everything."

Adrienne couldn't help being amused, though Gideon was scowling. "Even if one of Gideon's books is optioned for film, he and I would have little input into casting, Carla. But I would certainly pass your suggestions along."

"Maybe he could be in one of those cameo spots, like other writers have done. I've always told him he's got the looks for Hollywood, even if he could use some work in the personality department." She laughed heartily at her own wit as she patted Gideon's shoulder with a familiarity that Adrienne would bet few others dared to display.

"I've told you before I have no secret desire to see myself onscreen, Carla."

Ignoring Gideon's grumble, Carla continued to Adrienne, "Maybe Hollywood will put a little more romance in his stories. I told Gideon all those thrills and chills in his last book were fine, but it wouldn't hurt him to put in a little more sizzle."

"You do have other customers, Carla. Go tell them all you've learned and conjectured about my business." Gideon's words were gruff, but Adrienne thought she heard the faintest undertone of affection.

Perhaps Carla heard it, as well. She didn't seem to take offense, but merely laughed again. Before she moved on, she said, "You have a pleasant visit in Honesty, Miz Corley. Have Gideon show you some of the sights around here before you go back to the big city."

"*Are* there any sights around here?" Adrienne couldn't resist asking when the waitress moved on.

"I suppose that's in the eye of the beholder." He glanced at her empty plate. "Are you finished?"

"Yes." His own plate was also empty, she noted. Amazing.

Attention focused on them again as they made their way across the diner toward the cash register. Because she didn't want a public scene, and suspected Gideon did not share that qualm, she didn't argue with him when he pulled out his wallet and gave her a look that dared her to object.

Once again she noted that the greetings he exchanged with those around him could hardly be described as warm or encouraging. Didn't he *have* friends around here?

As they stepped out of the diner, they almost collided with a uniformed police officer who was just entering. He smiled apologetically at Adrienne, and she was struck by how attractive he was in a rough, sexy sort of way. Talk about film-star material...

And then he spotted Gideon. His face hardened, and his

smile vanished. Gideon stiffened beside her, and she could almost feel the temperature drop by several degrees.

"You always seem to be standing in my way, Mc-Cloud," the officer drawled, a rather dangerous edge to his deep voice.

"You could always leave town and avoid any risk of running into me," Gideon replied evenly.

Adrienne lifted an eyebrow in response to the blatant antagonism between these two men who seemed to be very close to the same age. "Perhaps we should all step to our right and clear a path," she said when neither appeared willing to move.

The officer gave her a nod and moved out of the way, sweeping his hand in a polite gesture obviously intended for her. "Ladies first."

Placing a warning hand on Gideon's arm—after all, it was her job to look out for him, in a manner of speaking—she smiled and practically towed Gideon outside with her. "Thank you, officer," she said over her shoulder.

"My pleasure, ma'am."

Gideon made a sound that might have been a growl, followed by a muttered, "Jerk."

"Always a delight to see you, too, McCloud," the other man called after them.

Adrienne felt a ripple of anger run through Gideon's arm before she dropped her hand. "Old friend?" she asked dryly.

Gideon merely gave her a look and stalked toward her rental car.

Chapter Three

Fifteen minutes after they returned to Gideon's house—
just after 9:30 a.m.—Adrienne found herself alone in his
kitchen. After telling her he needed to work on a scene
while it was still fresh in his mind, he'd closed himself in
his office again. He'd looked relieved when she'd assured
him she had brought quite a bit of reading with her, since
she couldn't even take a vacation without having her work
nearby, and he'd promised to be out to talk business with
her as soon as he finished the scene.

She had decided she'd better not hold her breath until
he reemerged. Settling at the kitchen table with her laptop
computer, her cell phone and a stack of manuscripts, she
concentrated on her work as diligently as she assumed Gideon was concentrating on his.

It was rather nice, actually, to work uninterrupted for a
change. Vacation time or not, she might actually get quite

a lot accomplished on this trip—if only she could convince Gideon to cooperate.

Gideon was aware of Adrienne's presence in his house. She didn't make any noise, even though he found himself listening for her on several occasions, but he knew she was there, anyway. The awareness didn't stop him from working—or even from losing himself in his writing—but each time he surfaced, he thought of Adrienne.

Not such terribly intrusive thoughts to have, he acknowledged, picturing her brown eyes and glossy auburn hair. And then his imagination drifted a bit lower, lingering on her sleek, slender curves. Willowy, he decided. That was the word he would have chosen to describe her.

Maybe it wasn't such a bad thing having a willowy woman in the next room while he worked. As soon as he finished this scene, he would go talk to her....

It was just after eleven when the kitchen telephone rang, drawing Adrienne out of her work. She glanced up as it rang again. Surely Gideon would answer.

The phone rang again. Shaking her head at his refusal to buy an answering machine if he had no intention of picking up the phone, she pushed herself out of her chair and stalked toward the extension. *Someone* had to answer. This could be an emergency. "McCloud residence," she said.

After a momentary pause, a woman spoke. "This is Lenore McCloud, Gideon's mother. May I ask to whom I'm speaking?"

"I'm Adrienne Corley, Mrs. McCloud. Gideon's agent from New York."

"I see. Was my son expecting your visit? He didn't mention it to me."

"I'm afraid I popped in unexpectedly," Adrienne explained. "I had some important business to discuss with him and I, um, had a bit of difficulty reaching him to arrange a meeting."

His mother's laugh was wry. "That I believe. Reaching Gideon is an impossible task at times. I wasn't sure he would answer this call, even though he surely knew I would be checking in with him."

"I'll go tell him you're on the line. He's in his office."

"Oh, dear. I hope he doesn't snap at you."

"You needn't worry about my feelings being hurt if he does." Adrienne thought ruefully of her father. "I'm quite used to that sort of thing."

"Well...good luck."

Adrienne thought she might like Gideon's mother, but then she'd already decided the woman must have the forbearance of a saint to put up with Gideon and to accept her ex-husband's child so graciously. "Thank you."

Laying the receiver on the kitchen counter, she walked to Gideon's office and knocked firmly on the door, knowing a tentative tap would probably never catch his attention. She didn't wait for an invitation to enter, but opened the door and stuck her head inside. "Gideon, your mother is on the phone."

He didn't take his eyes from his computer screen. "Tell her I'll call her later."

"No, you won't, you'll forget. You really should talk to her now while she's on the line."

It was the same rational tone she used with her father when he was acting unreasonably. Sometimes the strategy worked, and sometimes it just ticked him off.

Gideon seemed on the verge of the latter as he glared at her. And then he shook his head, pushed a hand through his hair and muttered, "Sorry. I get surly when my flow of thought is interrupted."

"No problem. I'm often the same way. Are you taking the call in here?"

He nodded and reached for the phone.

"I'll hang up the extension in the kitchen," she said, and let herself out of his office, closing the door behind her.

He wasn't an entirely hopeless case, she decided as she slipped the receiver quietly into its cradle and returned to her own work. He just needed someone to take him in hand and remind him about the manners his mother had no doubt tried to instill in him. Not that she had any interest in taking on such a project herself, of course.

"She sounds nice."

Half his attention still focused on the words on his computer screen, Gideon frowned. "Yes, she's nice. And, no, nothing interesting is going on here. She's here to discuss business with me—which we're going to do as soon as I finish this scene I've been struggling with for days."

"Yes, I know you want to get back to work," his mother said with long-suffering resignation. "I simply wanted to check on things there. Did Isabelle sleep well? Did you have any trouble getting her to school this morning?"

"As far as I know, she slept just fine. And she was only a few minutes late to school, which hardly justified the attitude I got from the old biddy who runs the place. It's preschool, for crying out loud. What's the kid going to miss if she's a few minutes late? Advanced coloring class?"

"Miss Thelma can be a bit...unbending," Lenore acknowledged. "But she means well, Gideon. She's an excellent administrator, and you can certainly understand that having her students there on time makes her schedule run more smoothly. Please try to be patient with her until I return, for Isabelle's sake.''

"When *are* you coming home?'' he asked without making any guarantees about his patience. "How's Aunt Wanda?''

"Not good, I'm afraid. She went into shock before she was found, and you know her heart is bad. She's in intensive care now.''

"I'm sorry to hear that,'' he said, and the words were sincere. Though he wasn't close to his maternal aunt, he knew his mother must be frantic with worry about her only sister. And, though he rarely expressed his feelings, he cared very deeply about his mother. "Do you need me to come there to help you with anything?'' he offered a bit awkwardly.

"No, darling, but thank you for offering.'' Lenore sounded genuinely touched. "I know you're busy with your book, and to be honest, the best thing you can do to help me now is to take care of Isabelle. I would hate to have to call Nathan and Caitlin home early from their honeymoon, unless it's absolutely necessary.''

"She's no trouble at all,'' Gideon said, especially with Adrienne here to help out, he silently added. He wondered how much longer he could delay his agent's return to New York. After all, wasn't it part of her job to make sure he finished his books in a timely manner?

"I'll call again tomorrow,'' Lenore said. "And answer the telephone, will you? It could be an emergency at Isabelle's school, you know.''

He grimaced. "I'll try to listen for it,'' he promised without enthusiasm.

He was definitely going to have to buy an answering machine.

He couldn't have said how much time passed before his work was interrupted again, by yet another knock on the office door. Scowling, he looked around. "What now?"

Adrienne opened the door. "Sorry to interrupt again, but didn't you say Isabelle gets out of school at two?"

"Yeah. Why?" He glanced at his watch. It was already one-thirty. "Damn. I'm finally close to finishing this scene."

"Why don't I go get her? The booster seat is still in my car, and I remember the way."

Tempted, he glanced from her to the screen again. "You're sure it wouldn't be too much trouble?"

"Not at all. Of course, you'd better call the school first and see if it's okay. I'm a stranger to the staff. We can't expect them to turn Isabelle over to me without authorization."

He reached for the phone. Five minutes and a few terse exchanges later, they had their approval. "You'll have to show your driver's license and this note," he said, scrawling something on a sheet of unlined paper. "But you're authorized."

She plucked the signed note from his fingers. "I'm on my way. It's a good thing I brought an umbrella with me."

Only then did he become aware of the steady drumming rain against the office windows. "How long has it been raining?"

"Almost an hour. According to the radio in your kitchen, we're in for some downpours this afternoon and early evening."

"You'll be okay picking up Isabelle?"

"I'll be fine. Finish your scene. You and I really need

to talk business today. I have to get back to New York tomorrow.''

He nodded. ''We'll talk as soon as you get back.''

She really was being very helpful with Isabelle, he thought after she left, as he stretched a few kinks out of his shoulders. As eager as he was to get back to his normal routines, he rather wished Adrienne could stay as long as Isabelle did. He was sure that was the only reason he was so reluctant to see her return to New York.

Listening to the steady fall of rain outside the office windows, he frowned, wondering if he should have insisted on going after Isabelle himself. He hoped Adrienne wouldn't have any problems picking her up. And then he reminded himself that Adrienne had a stake in his finishing this book—after all, she didn't get paid until he did.

He put his hands to the keyboard again and let himself be drawn back into the world that existed solely in his mind.

Emerging from her colorfully decorated classroom with a stream of other students, Isabelle greeted Adrienne with a bright smile. ''Hi, Miss Corley. Did you come for me?''

Adrienne returned the smile, pleased that the child seemed happy to see her. ''Yes. Your brother is busy writing, so I volunteered.''

Thelma Fitzpatrick, the gruff-voiced, squarely built owner of Miss Thelma's Preschool and Daycare, hovered nearby with a frown on her irritable-grandmother face. ''This is highly unorthodox,'' she grumbled. ''We are not accustomed to releasing our students to complete strangers.''

Since Adrienne had already provided Gideon's letter of authorization and her driver's license, she didn't know what else it would take to reassure the woman. ''I respect

your concern for your students, Mrs. Fitzpatrick. I know
the McClouds must have the utmost confidence that Isabelle is safe here.''

The woman folded her hands in front of her and eyed
Adrienne with lingering suspicion. "I suppose we've done
all we can, considering that her guardian is off on his hon-
eymoon and her appointed caretaker had to leave town.
Though I can't imagine anyone leaving a small child with
Gideon McCloud," she added in a murmured aside.

Immediately defensive on Gideon's behalf—after all, he
was her client—she smiled coolly. "Actually, I think she's
in very good hands with her brother.''

"Humph." The other woman was notably unimpressed.
"You obviously don't know him very well.''

"Gideon's taking good care of me, Miss Thelma," Isabelle said earnestly, proving she had been playing close
attention to the conversation. "He made me spaghetti for
dinner last night.''

"Yes, well…'' Miss Thelma cleared her throat. "Go
with Ms. Corley, Isabelle. I'll see you in the morning. And
don't forget to bring a stuffed animal for our jungle party.''

"I won't forget." Demonstrating that she wasn't particularly intimidated by the stern-looking woman, Isabelle
gave her a big hug before skipping out of the school at
Adrienne's side.

Sheltering the little girl beneath her umbrella, Adrienne
ushered her to the car and secured her into the booster seat
in the back. Isabelle started babbling about her day the
minute Adrienne slid behind the steering wheel. Trying to
concentrate on the child's chatter and negotiate the wet
roads at the same time, Adrienne murmured what she
hoped were appropriate responses. Isabelle must have been
satisfied, since she continued with barely a pause for
breath.

Cute kid, Adrienne thought with a faint smile, but the child did love to talk.

A traffic light glowed red ahead of her as she approached the last intersection before leaving the city limits. It changed to green several seconds before she reached it, so she didn't slow down. The nose of the rental car had just entered the intersection when a blur of red passed in front of her, so close she could almost feel the heat of its exhaust.

She slammed on the brakes, missing a collision by a heartbeat. The lightweight rental car slid on the wet pavement, squealing into a spin that she fought with her heart pounding in her throat. The spin ended with a crunch of metal when the back of the car made jarring contact with a lamppost. Her hands white-knuckled on the steering wheel, Adrienne sat for a moment in frozen silence, trying to remember how to breathe again. And then a wail from the back seat got her moving.

She whipped around in her seat. "Isabelle, are you all right?"

Still strapped securely in her safety seat, the little girl was uninjured, though she was obviously frightened. Going limp with relief, Adrienne swallowed hard before saying, "It's okay, sweetheart. The car's a little crumpled, but you and I are fine. You don't hurt anywhere, do you?"

Drawing in a tremulous breath, Isabelle shook her head. "I'm not hurt."

"Good." Because the child still appeared to be in need of comfort, Adrienne reached for the door handle. "Hold on just a minute. I'll come around to you."

The rain had dwindled to barely more than a mist. Adrienne didn't bother with an umbrella, figuring that after what they had just been through, a little moisture certainly wouldn't hurt either of them. No other vehicles were immediately visible when she stepped out of the driver's door, though she could hear a car engine approaching on the intersecting street. She hoped whoever it was would call for assistance while she comforted Isabelle. She had carelessly left her own cell phone sitting on Gideon's kitchen table.

Opening the rear passenger door, she reached inside to unbuckle Isabelle, who had stopped sniffling, but still looked shaken. The child wrapped her arms around Adrienne's neck and buried her face in her throat. "I was scared."

Adrienne rocked her soothingly, an instinctive movement that somehow seemed appropriate. "So was I, sweetheart."

Fear was rapidly changing to anger for her. That moron in the red car could have killed them! And he hadn't even stayed around to see if anyone was hurt.

The vehicle she'd heard approaching stopped at the traffic light, then turned to slide in behind her car. She wouldn't have to ask anyone to call the police, after all. The police had already arrived, she thought, relieved to see the marked patrol car. She was even more surprised to recognize the officer who exited the vehicle and moved toward her. He was the same man she'd almost bumped into that morning when she and Gideon left the diner.

"Are you all right, ma'am?" he asked her in the rough-edged drawl she remembered from earlier.

"Yes, we're okay. Just shaken."

He studied the crumpled rear of the nondescript compact. "What happened? Did you hydroplane?"

Her temper flared again. "Some jerk in a red sports car ran a red light right in front of me! If I hadn't practically stood on the brakes, I would have slammed right into him."

The officer's cool gray eyes narrowed. "A red sports car?"

She nodded, uncertain whether he believed her or not. "He was driving like a maniac—speeding and swerving. He didn't even slow down to see if we were okay."

"You didn't get a look at the license plate, did you?"

"No. Everything happened too quickly."

"Doesn't matter. I know who it was. Not much I can do about it without another witness, but you can bet I'll let him know I heard about this."

She doubted that would accomplish much, but she supposed she had little recourse. She couldn't even tell him the make of the vehicle, and he couldn't go around questioning everyone in town who drove a red sports car, even though he seemed to think he already knew who'd been driving like such a maniac. A repeat offender, apparently.

"You're both getting wet in this mist. Why don't we sit in the patrol car while I fill out the accident report and call for a wrecker?"

"You really think a wrecker is necessary?"

"Ma'am, you won't be driving that car anywhere. The back fender is crumpled all around the rear tire."

She sighed. Terrific. She hoped her insurance company and the rental car service would be able to work all this out without much trouble. Running a hand over Isabelle's damp hair, she moved toward the cruiser. "I appreciate your assistance, Officer…?"

"Smith, ma'am. Dylan Smith." He touched the brim of his hat in a rather charmingly old-fashioned gesture.

"I'm Adrienne Corley."

"Yes, I know. You're Gideon McCloud's agent from New York. Heard all about you from Carla at the diner this morning." He opened the back passenger door of the patrol car. "Your pretty little friend can sit in the back seat while you and I fill out the accident report in the front."

"Would you like to sit in the police car, Isabelle?"

The child looked intrigued. "Okay." She climbed obligingly into the car, leaning over the front seat to study the dashboard and radio.

"I suppose I'll need my identification and insurance policy number. Would you mind keeping an eye on Isabelle while I get my purse?"

"Not at all, ma'am."

As Adrienne made her way across the slick pavement toward the crumpled car, she wondered if Dylan Smith deliberately tried to act the stereotype of a drawling Southern cop. She still didn't know the root of his antagonism toward Gideon, or vice versa, since Gideon hadn't mentioned the encounter again after leaving the diner, but Officer Smith had been pleasant enough to her. Apparently he didn't hold her association with Gideon against her.

She had just reached the front of the rental car when her foot came down on an oily pool of rain water. The slick sole of her loafer offered absolutely no traction. Her leg flew out from under her, and she felt herself falling.

All she could do was brace herself for the impact with the hard, wet pavement.

Gideon's sneakers slapped hard against the floor tiles of the Honesty Medical Clinic. Staff and patients alike moved swiftly out of his path as he charged down the hallway to the emergency examining room. No one dared interfere with his progress.

Sitting on a padded bench in the hallway outside the closed door of the examining room, Isabelle was happily listening to her own heartbeat through a stethoscope as a brightly uniformed young brunette hovered nearby. The child smiled broadly when she spotted her brother. "Hi, Gideon."

He knelt in front of her, his hand on her knee as he looked for injuries. "Are you all right?"

She nodded. "We had a wreck, but nobody got hurt, and then Miss Corley fell down and Officer Smith brought us here, but Miss Corley's going to be okay and Miss Nancy's letting me listen through a stefascope."

"It's a stethoscope, Isabelle," the young woman corrected clearly.

"Stethoscope," the child parroted carefully.

Nancy beamed at Gideon. "She's so bright. I can't believe she's only—"

"Where's Adrienne?" he broke in, having reassured himself that Isabelle was unharmed.

Nancy's smile faded a bit in response to his curt interruption. "She's in there with the doctor. But you can't—"

Gideon pushed open the examining room door and moved through it, leaving Nancy sputtering behind him as the door swung closed in her face.

Wearing a hospital gown with a thin robe belted over it, Adrienne sat at one end of a paper-covered examining table, her bare feet dangling over the end. Her right foot was strapped into a black brace, her bare toes notably swollen. Two women stood at one side of the room studying a chart; Gideon recognized one as the doctor and assumed the other was a nurse.

It was the uniformed police officer hovering very close to Adrienne's side, smiling at her and being smiled at in return, who sent Gideon's blood pressure soaring.

He knew he was glowering when Adrienne looked his way, but she didn't seem particularly intimidated by his forbidding expression. Her smile turned rueful. "I'm afraid I've done something stupid."

Gideon moved to Adrienne's side, effectively stepping between her and Dylan Smith. "Are you all right?"

She gestured toward her injured foot. "The good news is that my ankle isn't broken, only badly sprained. And Isabelle is fine."

"Yes, I saw her out in the hallway. What happened?"

"Someone ran a red light and almost caused a collision, then took off without stopping. I went into a spin and hit a streetlamp pole."

"That's when you hurt your foot?"

Glancing down at her hands, she cleared her throat. "No. I, er, slipped and fell on the wet pavement, landing with my foot twisted beneath me." She raised her eyes to smile gratefully at Dylan, who had stepped back but still stood nearby. "Officer Smith handled everything beautifully. He called for a wrecker, then brought me straight here without alarming Isabelle. I don't know what I would have done if he hadn't come along when he did."

Something about the way she smiled at the officer made Gideon's hands itch to curl into fists. He glared at the other man. "Shouldn't you be out arresting someone for causing an accident and then leaving the scene?"

"I wish I could," Dylan replied evenly. "Unfortunately, Ms. Corley was the only witness, and she didn't get a good look at the other vehicle."

"All I saw was a speeding red sports car," Adrienne confirmed. "Everything happened too fast for me to get a license plate number or even the make of the car."

"A red sports car?" Gideon turned to Dylan again. "You're telling me you don't know who that was?"

"You and I both know it was probably Kirk Sawyer," Dylan answered with obviously forced patience. "But he doesn't drive the only red car in town. Without a license plate number or some identification, my hands are tied.''

Gideon made a sound of disgust. "Figures."

Dylan's eyes narrowed in corresponding anger. Adrienne spoke quickly. "Officer Smith has done all he can to help me, Gideon. I'm very grateful to him.''

Dylan faced Adrienne, deliberately turning a shoulder to Gideon. "I'm glad I was able to help, ma'am. You be sure and call me if there's anything else I can do for you while you're in town.''

Gideon was disgusted by the way Adrienne seemed to be taken in by the other man's exaggerated Southern charm. "Thank you, Officer," she said sweetly.

He nodded and donned the hat he'd been holding. "Take care of that ankle, ma'am.'' Turning toward the doorway, he raked Gideon with a cool look. "McCloud,'' he muttered in lieu of a more civil leave-taking.

Gideon focused on Adrienne again, effectively dismissing the departing officer. "When can you leave?''

The doctor stepped forward then, having discreetly stayed out of the way during Gideon's terse conversation with Dylan. "She can go as soon as she's dressed and I've talked to her a bit more about the care of her ankle. I'm lending her a pair of crutches she can use for a few days just to make walking more comfortable.''

Gideon glanced at Adrienne. "I'll go wait with Isabelle while you get dressed.''

"Be sure and let her know I'm fine, even though I'll be using crutches when I join you. I don't want her to be worried.''

"I'll tell her.'' Nodding toward the doctor and nurse, he turned and left the room, impatient to get out of this place and back to his own house.

Isabelle was still sitting on the bench with the young

clinic employee, this time playing with a tongue depressor. "I saw her tonsils," she announced proudly to Gideon.

"Congratulations. You seem to be well on your way to becoming a doctor." He sat on the bench beside his sister and directed a faint smile at her companion. "Thanks for keeping her entertained. I'll take over now so you can get back to work."

The brunette nodded. "Okay. 'Bye, Isabelle. You've been a very good girl."

Isabelle flashed her numerous dimples in one of her particularly endearing smiles. "'Bye, Nancy."

And then she turned to Gideon. "Where's Miss Corley?"

"She's getting ready to go home with us."

"Is her leg okay? She fell and hurt it and Officer Smith carried her to his police car."

The image of Adrienne being carried in Dylan's arms almost made Gideon scowl again. He kept his expression bland only because he didn't want to upset Isabelle. "Adrienne hurt her ankle, and she'll be wearing a brace until it heals. She'll walk with crutches for a few days to keep her weight off the injury until it feels better."

Isabelle looked concerned. "Does it hurt?"

"I'm sure it's uncomfortable, but she was smiling when I was in there with her." Mostly at Dylan Smith, he couldn't help remembering with another ripple of irritation.

Isabelle seemed to be reassured. "I can take care of her when we get to your house," she offered. "I can bring things to her so she won't have to walk on her hurt foot."

"Adrienne will appreciate your help."

He was startled when Isabelle suddenly climbed onto

his lap and rested her head on his chest. "I'm kind of tired," she murmured with a little sigh.

Awkwardly patting her back, he wasn't surprised that she was worn-out. She'd had a long, eventful day.

He was beginning to feel rather drained himself.

Chapter Four

Her swollen and bruised foot propped on a pillow on a footstool in front of her chair, Adrienne sat in Gideon's den that evening with a cup of hot tea in her hands and a white stuffed owl in her lap. Gideon and Isabelle had been taking care of her, in their unique ways, which explained the tea and the toy.

She still felt like a fool.

Poor Gideon, she thought, listening to the clatter of dishes in the kitchen as he cleared away the remains of the broiled steak and baked potato dinner he had prepared for them. All he seemed to want was to be left alone to write in peace, and now he found himself responsible for his baby sister and his injured agent.

Gideon wandered into the den a few moments later. "You need anything?"

"No, I'm fine, thank you. I was just thinking that I should try calling the airline, see if I can get a flight out early tomorrow. I'll have to arrange transportation to the airport, of course, since I'm not sure I could make an hour-long drive with my right foot in a brace, but I—''

"That's ridiculous. You're in no shape to travel tomorrow. The doctor ordered you to take it easy for a few days and that's what you'll do. Stay here and recuperate, and you can go back to New York later in the week. Friday, probably.''

Though she appreciated his generous, if bluntly offered, invitation, especially knowing how badly he wanted his privacy back, she shook her head. "Thank you, but I won't impose on you any longer. I'm not injured that badly, and I can get assistance boarding the plane.''

He crossed his arms over his chest and glared at her. "I'm not going to argue with you about this. You're going to be sore tomorrow, both from the impact in the car and from the fall. There's no reason for you to leave in that condition—and don't say again that you don't want to impose on me. I would tell you if I found your presence bothersome.''

"I should never have shown up on your doorstep without giving you prior notice.''

Her guiltfest only seemed to annoy him further. "You didn't have a hell of a lot of choice, considering I wouldn't take your calls or read my mail.''

Now he was making excuses for her. She sighed and shook her head. "I'm really sorry about all of this.''

"If anyone should be apologizing, I should, for making your job so difficult. I haven't even made time to discuss the business that brought you here. But it would be a waste of time for us to sit here apologizing to each other.''

She smiled ruefully. "I suppose you're right. And I know how you feel about wasting time.''

The smile he gave her in return was a bit lopsided, but

still charming in its own way. For an instant she was taken back to the moment when she had stepped out of the examining room and found Gideon waiting for her with Isabelle curled in his lap. He had looked more than a bit uncomfortable, but his hand had been gentle as he'd patted Isabelle's back. She had been startled to find herself wondering how it might feel to have his hands on *her.*

"You seem to be getting to know me pretty well," he said.

It took her a beat to realize that he was responding to her last statement and not to her errant thoughts. She cleared her throat. "In some ways, perhaps."

He sat on the couch, draping his arm over the back. "How's your tea?"

"It's very good." She took a sip of the cooling, interestingly flavored beverage.

"It's my mother's favorite herbal blend. She keeps me stocked because she thinks I drink too much caffeine."

"Do you?"

"Probably."

"Where's Isabelle?"

He glanced toward the doorway. "In my office. She wanted to draw pictures."

"She really is an amazing child. I know she's only four, but she acts so much older. Her mannerisms, her vocabulary…everything about her."

"She's spent almost all her life around adults. Her parents spent nearly every waking moment with her before they died. After that she lived with her maternal great-aunt in California for a few months until her aunt became ill and turned her over to my brother. I believe this preschool program is the first time she's ever really been around other kids."

"She's had a lot of tragedy in her short life, hasn't she?" Adrienne murmured quietly.

His face expressionless, Gideon nodded. "She'll have a good home with Nathan and Caitlin. The three of them are crazy about each other. But then, Isabelle has known Nathan all her life, so she'd already bonded with him before she moved here."

A bit confused, Adrienne frowned. "She hasn't known you all her life?"

He looked toward the doorway again, so that all she could see of his face was the hard line of his jaw. "My father and I didn't get along very well even before he dumped my mother and moved to California with his pregnant girlfriend, who he married just before Isabelle's birth. I hadn't seen him since he moved. He died in a tourist helicopter crash in Mexico last year."

The very lack of emotion in his voice made her throat tighten. Though he wouldn't let it surface, she suspected he still harbored a great deal of emotion about his father— anger, an equal amount of pain and probably a few regrets. Because of her complicated and frequently acrimonious relationship with her own father, she could identify with his mixed emotions. The difference was that she still had some hope of settling things between her father and herself. Gideon's last chance was gone.

He nodded toward her elevated foot, abruptly changing the subject. "How's your ankle?"

"Sore," she admitted, trying not to dwell on the discomfort.

"Need another pain pill? I think it's time for you to take one now."

"I'd rather not. They make me woozy."

"Isn't it better to be woozy than in pain?"

"It's not so bad," she lied, shifting her foot gingerly on the pillow. "I'll put some more ice on it before I turn in."

"Maybe now is a good time to discuss the business that brought you here." He looked as though he would rather undergo a root canal, but she could tell he was trying to feign interest for her sake.

She nodded and began. "I had a long lunch with your editor last week, and she—"

"Miss Corley! I made you a get-well picture." Waving a sheet of paper in front of her, Isabelle dashed into the room. "I drew a bunch of them before I decided which one I liked best."

Adrienne made a point of admiring and praising the colorful, imaginative picture of rainbows and flowers and smiling animals that were certainly creative, if a bit hard to identify. The drawing was painstakingly signed with Isabelle's name. "This is lovely, Isabelle. I'll treasure it. Thank you."

Dimpling, Isabelle leaned over the arm of Adrienne's chair to give her a hug. "Does it make you feel better?"

Adrienne returned the hug with an unexpected rush of affection. "Much better."

Satisfied, Isabelle turned then to Gideon. "I'm still sort of hungry. Could I have a cookie for dessert?"

He pushed himself off the couch. "How about two cookies and a glass of milk?"

She clapped her hands. "Yummy. Do you want a cookie, Miss Corley? I'll bring you one so you don't have to walk."

"No, thank you, sweetheart. I'm still full from dinner."

"Okay. See you later." She skipped out of the room at Gideon's side.

Adrienne studied the drawing in her hand with a smile. No one had ever drawn a picture for her before. It was such a sweet gesture. She'd been completely honest when she'd told Isabelle that she would treasure this gift.

She had grown very fond of little Isabelle in the twenty-four hours she'd known her. And she was becoming more fascinated by Gideon with each passing hour.

Leaning her head against the back of the chair, she reflected on the awkward situation she had gotten herself into. She was not by nature an impulsive or impractical person. She rarely acted without detailed planning and clearly defined goals. This trip to Honesty definitely qualified as impulsive, even though she had decided to take it several days before her departure. She'd made up her mind in an instant and hadn't allowed herself to second-guess the decision afterward, even though she had been aware that it wasn't the most rational business move she'd ever made.

And now, twenty-four hours after her arrival, she'd made absolutely no progress in discussing business with Gideon. To make matters worse, she had injured herself and was proving to be an inconvenience to him. This was what she deserved, she supposed, for losing her patience and her temper and behaving so uncharacteristically.

Because she didn't want to spend any more time alone with her recriminations, she reached for the crutches beside her chair. There was pain when she lowered her foot from the stool and rose, but she ignored it. Following the doctor's instructions, she moved her injured foot in a walking motion, though she put little weight on it as she made her way carefully to the kitchen.

Isabelle sat at the table, swinging her feet and talking while she crumbled cookies on a plate. Most of the pieces made it to her mouth, but she seemed more interested in telling Gideon a lengthy and complex tale about her classmates' playground antics than in eating her dessert.

Gideon leaned against the counter, solemnly munching a cookie and trying to follow Isabelle's monologue. He looked relieved when Adrienne entered, a bit as if he'd heard the welcome call of a cavalry bugle, she thought with a faint smile. And then he frowned. "What are you doing up? I'd have brought you anything you needed."

"I was getting restless. I'm not used to sitting still for so long." She moved toward the cabinet where he stored his drinking glasses. "Since I'm already up, I'd like a glass of water."

He reached over her shoulder for a glass, brushing against her with the movement. She was keenly aware of the feel of his muscled arm against her shoulder. "Do you want ice?" he asked, his voice a low growl in her ear.

She hadn't been particularly warm before she'd entered the kitchen. She was now. "Yes, please."

He looked at her for a moment, and she wondered if the contact between them had affected him, too. Or was he simply reading something in her expression? Before she could decide, he turned to the side-by-side refrigerator and opened the freezer door.

She jumped when the telephone rang. The extension was on the wall right beside her. Busily filling her glass with ice, Gideon glanced her way. "I suppose you think we should answer that."

"Of course."

"Would you mind? If it's a telemarketer, tell him he can—"

She cleared her throat loudly and looked warningly toward his attentive little sister. And then, balancing on her crutches, she reached for the receiver. "McCloud residence."

She'd half expected to hear his mother on the other end

of the line again. Instead it was a man who said, "Is, um, Gideon there? This is his brother, Nathan."

"Just a moment." She extended the receiver toward Gideon. "It's your brother."

Isabelle's face brightened. "It's Nate? Can I say hi?"

"Of course you can," Gideon assured her, trading Adrienne a glass of water for the phone. "Hang on a minute."

Adrienne set the water on the table, then carefully lowered herself into a chair to drink it. Just that brief walk from the den had left her foot burning with pain. The doctor had assured her the discomfort would lessen in a few days, especially if she took care of it and eased into the exercises she'd been given, but tonight the pain was intense. Not that she would admit that, of course. She'd caused Gideon enough concern.

She couldn't help overhearing his side of his conversation with his brother as she sipped her water. Isabelle listened openly, squirming in her seat to signal her impatience to have a turn at the telephone.

"That was my agent," Gideon said, sounding resigned to explaining Adrienne's presence yet again. "She's spending a few days here on business.... Yes, I'm being hospitable," he added crossly in response to something his brother said.

"Isabelle's fine," he said a moment later. "You can ask her yourself. She wants to talk to you.... No, there's no reason to cut your honeymoon short. I can handle things here until Mom gets back."

There was another pause, and then Gideon spoke gruffly again, "That's not necessary. You'd do the same for me. Here, talk to Isabelle. She's about to explode."

Hopping down from her chair in response to Gideon's motion, Isabelle took the phone in her eager little hands. "Hi, Nate. I'm not really going to explode. Gideon was joking. Are you having fun on your honeymoon? Is Caitlin having fun, too? I lost Hedwig last night, but Miss Corley helped me find him. She's nice and she's pretty, too.''

Gideon pulled the chair he'd settled into closer to Adrienne. ''I think you've got a fan,'' he murmured, keeping his voice low so he wouldn't distract Isabelle. Not that it seemed likely, since the child barely paused for breath before moving on to a recital of everything that happened at school that day.

Very aware of how closely he was sitting to her, she managed a smile. ''Your little sister certainly loves to talk.''

''I've noticed that. Funny, she's always been more reserved with me than with other people, but she seems to be getting over that.''

''Maybe she was waiting for a signal from you that you wanted to be her friend. She told me she didn't think you were used to having children around.''

''She was right about that. And I never expected to spend this much time with *her*.''

Glancing at Isabelle, who was still babbling happily into the telephone, Adrienne asked just as quietly, ''Don't you enjoy being with her?''

''It hasn't been too bad so far,'' he conceded. ''But you've been here to help me with her almost since she arrived. That's made it a lot easier.''

She cast a rueful glance at the crutches propped nearby. ''I don't know how you can say I've helped you, when all I've done is add to your problems.''

''Not true. I'm sorry you hurt your ankle, but you've actually been very helpful in keeping Isabelle entertained.''

He was trying to be nice, and because she sensed that

wasn't something he made an effort to do very often, she was touched.

"Gideon," Isabelle said then, "Nate wants to tell you goodbye."

Gideon nodded and rose to take the phone again. Adrienne wondered if it was simply accidental that his hand brushed her arm as he stood. The jolt of response deep in her stomach seemed out of proportion to the casual touch.

Maybe her pain was going to her head. Why else would she suddenly be so sensitive to every move Gideon made, every nuance of his expressions, every slight physical contact between them? Just the sound of his deep voice as he exchanged a few more words with his brother before disconnecting the call made little shivers of awareness course down her spine.

Maybe she should take a pain pill, after all. She seemed to be on the verge of becoming downright delirious.

Gideon had lived alone for quite a long time. Though he dated occasionally, he was rarely involved with anyone for more than a few months, and even during those brief liaisons, he had never invited anyone to spend the night in his home.

His privacy served as a barrier between himself and the complications of interpersonal relationships, romantic and familial. His life just seemed tidier that way and more easily controlled.

Because he was so accustomed to his solitary surroundings, he seemed particularly attuned to the slightest atypical noise. He was silently prowling the hallways at about two o'clock Wednesday morning, because he often paced when he had trouble sleeping, when he heard a sound from his bedroom. A moan, perhaps? A low whimper of pain?

Barefoot and shirtless, wearing nothing but a pair of

jeans, he hesitated a moment outside the closed door. Should he knock? Ask Adrienne if she was all right? But what if she was sleeping and he'd merely imagined the sound? She needed her rest. Besides which, the guest room was directly across the hallway, and he didn't want to wake Isabelle.

What did he know about this sort of thing, anyway? He was no caretaker. He'd never even had a pet.

He was just turning away from the bedroom door when he heard the sound again, and this time he was convinced it was, indeed, a soft moan. He reached for the doorknob, telling himself he would just peek in and make sure Adrienne was okay. After all, she was his guest and she had been injured. It was probably his duty as a host to check on her.

It was dark outside the room, but just enough moonlight filtered in through the sheer curtains to help him make his way to the bed. Adrienne was sleeping, but it was a fitful, restless slumber. She lay on her left side, her legs curled in front of her, and even as he watched, she shifted her right leg, making a very faint sound as she did so. She had refused the pain pills before turning in—she seemed to believe that even a couple of doses would turn her into an addict—and he suspected that her abused ankle was trying to make itself known even as she slept.

He slipped into the private master bathroom, filled a plastic cup with tap water and carried it back to the bed. The pill bottle was on the nightstand. Setting the cup beside it, he shook two of the small tablets into his palm. Only then did he lean over Adrienne and place a hand lightly on her shoulder. She wore a thin satin pajama top— he assumed there were matching bottoms beneath the sheets—and it seemed to him that she felt a bit too warm beneath the cool fabric. "Adrienne?"

She shifted beneath his touch. "Mmm?"

He gave her shoulder a gentle shake. "Adrienne, wake up. I want you to take these pills."

Even in the heavy shadows, he could see that she was frowning when she looked up at him. "What are you doing? What's wrong?"

"You seem to be in pain. These pills will help you rest more comfortably. Open your mouth."

It was a measure of her disorientation that she followed his instructions without protest, swallowing the pills with a few sips of water as he steadied the cup for her. He was trying to keep this impersonal, but he was all too aware that she was lying in his bed, warm and tousled and sleepily cooperative. She was an attractive, interesting and desirable woman, and he would have had to be made of stone not to respond physically to these intimate circumstances.

He might be a loner, but he was no monk.

Maybe it was the water that roused her to full consciousness. She shifted suddenly away from his helping hands and attempted to push herself upright. The movement must have jarred her injured leg; she gasped a little and went very still.

Placing a hand on her shoulder, he nudged her back down on the pillows. "Take it easy. You need to get some more sleep."

"How did you know my leg was hurting?" she asked huskily.

"I heard you moan in your sleep when I walked past the door. Thought I'd better check on you."

He didn't expect gushing gratitude for his solicitude, but he was a bit taken aback when she muttered crossly, "I really didn't need the pills. I would have been fine without them."

He reminded himself that he didn't like people hovering

over him when he was under the weather, either. He'd been told, in fact, that he was a nightmare of a patient, but she could have at least said thanks for caring that she'd been hurting. "Just lie back and let the pills kick in. You can yell at me for my presumption tomorrow after you've had a good night's sleep."

She gave a soft sigh and reached out to catch his arm when he would have moved away. "Gideon, I'm sorry if I sounded ungracious. It's just that I hate being incapacitated in any way. I'm used to taking care of myself."

He settled onto the edge of the bed again. "I understand that. I don't much like doing what I'm told, either, especially when it's for my own good."

That made her smile a little. "But I do appreciate you checking on me. It was very kind of you."

He glanced down at her hand, which still lay on his bare arm, and it occurred to him that he should probably get the hell out of there. Immediately, if not sooner. "I am not a particularly nice person," he felt the need to tell her. "You can ask anyone."

She responded to that with a soft laugh. "I prefer to make up my own mind about whether someone is nice."

He really needed to get out of there, before he did something stupid, like making a clumsy pass at his injured agent.

"Yeah, well, I just don't want you to get the wrong impression of me," he muttered, and shoved himself to his feet while he was still able to do so. "I'm basically surly and self-centered and I like being that way."

She still sounded amused when she nestled more deeply into the covers and murmured, "Good night, Gideon."

Feeling like a fool, he didn't look back as he made a beeline for the door. "'Night."

This was what he got, he told himself, for acting completely out of character and trying to take care of other people instead of himself. As soon as his mother returned to take Isabelle off his hands, and Adrienne had healed enough to make the trip back to New York, he was reclaiming his solitude.

"Gideon?" Isabelle's sleepy voice floated through the open doorway of the guest room. "Is that you?"

"Yes, Isabelle. Everything's fine, you can go back to sleep."

"Could I have a drink of water?"

He sighed heavily. "Hang on a minute. I'll bring you one."

And then, he vowed, he was going to lock himself in his office again. And he would stay there this time.

Chapter Five

It must have been the pain pills that made Adrienne sleep later than usual Wednesday morning. Even the bright sunlight from the window didn't rouse her. It was nearly 9:00 a.m. when she forced open her gritty eyes and peered at the clock. Normally she would be at her office by this time, wide awake and already inundated with calls and e-mail.

Pushing her hands through her hair, she eased upright, moving her right leg with care. Her ankle was still bruised and swollen upon inspection, but maybe just a little less sore than it had been? An experimental flex made her teeth clench. Okay, maybe not.

Rubbing the back of her neck, she wondered for a moment if she had dreamed Gideon's middle-of-the-night visit. Had he really sat rumpled and shirtless on the side of her bed, supporting her while she had washed down the pain pills? She remembered, if fuzzily, that his touch had been very gentle, though his voice had been characteristically gruff.

She went all warm inside just thinking about it.

It took her a while to shower and dress, since she was still barely able to put her weight on her ankle. Gideon had moved several items of clothing to his office and had been using the shower in the guest bathroom. She still felt rather guilty about taking his bed and bath, even though he'd brusquely insisted he didn't mind at all.

She'd thrown the clothes she'd worn yesterday into Gideon's washer last night. They had been damp and dirty from her fall. She was rapidly running out of clean clothes, but she still had one casual outfit she hadn't worn yet, a pair of black slacks and a black-and-white-patterned top. She slipped a black loafer on her left foot, but could only wear the black brace on her right. Using the crutches for balance, she left Gideon's room.

The kitchen was empty, but a covered plate sat on the counter. Lifting the lid, she found two large, golden-brown muffins oozing with blueberries. Apparently Gideon had stopped by the bakery again after taking Isabelle to school. Certain he had left these out for her, she poured herself a cup of coffee, set it on the table, then carried one of the muffins with her to a chair. Serving herself was quite a balancing act, but she managed.

She took her time drinking the coffee and eating the muffin, enjoying both immensely. She'd been hungrier than she'd realized, probably because she hadn't felt like eating much the night before. And she needed the time alone to prepare herself for seeing Gideon. If, of course, he ever emerged from his office.

He did, in fact, less than ten minutes later. She had just finished her breakfast and was trying to muster the energy to pull out her computer when Gideon entered the kitchen, carrying an empty coffee mug and wearing a rather ferocious frown in addition to his standard uniform of jeans and T-shirt. "How's your leg?"

"Better, thank you."

His narrowed eyes swept her face. "That's a lie."

"Not entirely. It is a little better."

Though he still looked skeptical, he grunted and moved toward the coffeemaker. "Don't you want your other muffin?" he asked, glancing at the plate.

"No, one was enough for me. It was delicious, by the way."

Snagging the remaining muffin, he nodded and headed toward the doorway again, his filled-to-the-brim coffee mug in his other hand. "I'll be in my office if you need me."

"Gideon?"

He paused with an expression that combined impatience and wariness. "What?"

"When are we going to discuss the offers from your publisher?"

"We'll get to it. As soon as I—"

"I know," she interrupted in resignation. "As soon as you finish the scene you're working on."

He looked at her a moment, then turned without another word and left the room. Adrienne stared after him thoughtfully. Something was different about him today. He was just as blunt as usual, but a bit more distant, perhaps. Did it have anything to do with last night? Had he, too, found that interlude a bit too…intimate for professional associates?

A telephone rang, distracting her from that line of thought. At first she thought it was Gideon's phone again. And then she realized it was her own cell phone, which was sitting on the counter beside her briefcase. Fumbling with the crutches, she got to it on the third ring. "Hello?"

"Sorry to interrupt the vacation."

Instantly recognizing the apologetic voice, Adrienne settled carefully back into her chair. "Hi, Jacqueline. What's up?"

"Your father wants to know where you put the tax file he gave you to look over."

"I gave it back to him."

"I thought you did, but he swears you didn't."

Adrienne rolled her eyes. "Look in his office, on the credenza behind his desk. It's the red file on the left side of the credenza in a pile of other papers."

"Thanks. I'll find it. So are you still in Mississippi?"

"Yes, I am."

"Are you making any progress with Herman the Hermit?"

Adrienne smiled ruefully at the nickname. "Not really, I'm afraid—though you are not to report that to my father, of course."

"Is Gideon McCloud as weird as we thought he would be?"

"He's not weird." Adrienne kept one eye on the kitchen doorway as she spoke. "Just very private. And very focused on his writing. At least, when he isn't having to deal with other people's crises."

Her own, for example.

"So will you be coming back to New York today?"

"Um." Looking down at her purply, swollen foot, she said, "No, I won't be back today."

"Really? So what *will* you be doing there in the backwoods of Mississippi?"

"Ah, recuperating, mostly," Adrienne mumbled. "But only for a few more days. I've actually gotten quite a bit of work done. I'll be sending you an e-mail later this morning with some things I need you to do for me, and a few letters you can mail—"

"Adrienne."

She sighed. "Yes?"

"From what, exactly, are you recuperating?"

"I was in a minor accident with my rental car, but—"

"Oh, my God, are you—?"

"I wasn't hurt in the accident," Adrienne said hastily. "It was afterward. I slipped and fell on wet pavement and sprained my ankle. I've been ordered to take it easy for a few days, so it's probably best if I don't try to make the trip home before Friday, but other than that, I'm fine."

"I'm so sorry you were hurt. Is there anything I can do for you? Besides the list you're sending me, of course."

"No, that's all. And, um, there's no need to mention this accident to my father. As far as he needs to know, I'm simply taking some vacation time. He didn't really expect to hear from me this week, anyway."

"He knows I'm calling you. I'll just tell him you sound fine, which you do, so it's not really a lie. I wouldn't want him to be too worried about you."

Jacqueline's dry tone didn't quite hide her cynicism. Adrienne's brusque reply did not entirely conceal a touch of wistfulness. "We both know he would be more likely to be annoyed with my carelessness than concerned for my health. But by all means, tell him I'm fine."

"You're sure you're okay there? I hate to think of you staying alone in some hotel room when you're injured."

"Actually, I'm not staying at a hotel. Mr. McCloud invited me to stay at his place for a few days."

"Oh? Would this be the old, ugly, married Mr. McCloud?"

Adrienne cleared her throat. She could lie to her father

with ease, but she'd never been able to deceive her friend and assistant. "No. This would be the young, good-looking, single Mr. McCloud."

"I see."

The way Jacqueline stretched out those two syllables made Adrienne add hastily, "His sister's staying here with us."

"Oh." Jacqueline sounded vaguely disappointed to hear that Adrienne's visit was being chaperoned. There was no need to tell her, of course, that Gideon's sister had just celebrated her fourth birthday.

She couldn't lie to Jacqueline, but she saw no reason to tell her every little detail of this interesting interlude with Gideon McCloud.

Deciding that it was entirely possible Gideon wouldn't reappear at all that day—at least until she reminded him about picking up Isabelle—Adrienne settled in his den with her foot elevated and her work spread around her. She had trouble concentrating on her reading, though. Her thoughts kept wandering back to that late-night visit from Gideon.

Why was she having so much trouble putting that out of her mind? She'd bet Gideon hadn't given it another thought. He probably hadn't given *her* another thought as he'd lost himself in his writing.

When the doorbell rang at midmorning, she hesitated only a moment before reaching for the crutches and moving to answer it. She was certainly making herself at home here, she thought wryly, but it wasn't as if Gideon would rush to open the door. He probably hadn't even heard the bell.

Officer Dylan Smith stood on the doorstep, his toast-brown hair tousled in the breeze, his Old-West handsome face creased with a lazy smile. With the studied courtesy she had come to expect from him, he touched a finger to the brim of his hat and drawled, "'Morning, ma'am. How's the leg today?"

"Better, thank you," she fibbed.

He held out his hand, opening the palm to reveal a purple plastic bead bracelet. "I found this is in the back of my patrol car this morning. Since I don't think it belongs to the drunk I hauled in for relieving himself on Mrs. Arnett's prized rose bushes, I thought maybe someone here would recognize it."

Laughing, Adrienne reached out to take the inexpensive bauble from him. "It's Isabelle's. I remember seeing it on her arm. Everything was so hectic yesterday, I don't think she's even missed it."

He looked down at her right foot, which was still noticeably swollen. "That looks painful."

"It hurts," she replied candidly. "But it really is getting better, I think."

"Are you taking the pain pills the doctor gave you?"

She was immediately transported back several hours, to a gravelly voice in the darkness and a pair of gentle hands supporting her as she swallowed her pills. Feeling the blood warm in her cheeks, she looked away from the officer and motioned toward the den. "I take the pills only when I'm forced to. Won't you come in, Officer Smith? I just made a fresh pot of coffee. Gideon guzzles it by the gallon."

His smile turned wry. "Thanks, but as much as I would enjoy the visit with you, I'd better decline. If McCloud were to see me in his house, drinking his coffee, I'd probably have to haul him in for assaulting an officer."

Adrienne shook her head. "I'm afraid I don't understand

the hostility between you two. Gideon hasn't told me what caused it.''

"Let's just say he never fancied me as a brother-in-law.'' His smile no longer reached his eyes, and Adrienne sensed that his ironic tone was intended to mask a tangle of old emotions he didn't want examined too closely. And then he stepped back and touched his hat again, falling back into his blandly polite Southern-cop routine. "I'm glad you're doing better, Ms. Corley. You be sure and give me a call if there's ever anything I can do for you.''

"Thank you, Officer Smith.''

He turned and strolled to his car, whistling cheerily as he went. Still part of the act, Adrienne decided as she watched him leave. Just what was Officer Dylan Smith hiding behind that good-old-boy grin?

"What the hell was *he* doing here?''

Adrienne turned to find Gideon looming behind her, glaring over her shoulder at the departing patrol car. She dangled the purple bracelet from her fingers. "He found this in his patrol car this morning. It's Isabelle's. Nice of him to go to the trouble of returning it, wasn't it?''

Gideon's scowl only deepened. "He could have put it in the mail.''

Adrienne closed the door. "He said he also wanted to make sure I was okay. I thought that was very considerate of him.''

"I'm sure you did. Smith has always had a way of charming unsuspecting women.''

Using her crutches to make her way across the room, she lowered herself onto the couch again. "Did you date his sister or did he date yours?''

"Dylan doesn't have a sister.''

"He dated yours, then.''

Gideon planted his fists on his hips. "What did he say to you?"

"Only that you didn't fancy him as a brother-in-law."

Snorting, he dropped his arms. "Marriage was hardly in his plans for my younger sister."

Thinking about the emotions swirling in the officer's hard gray eyes, Adrienne murmured, "Are you so sure about that?"

After only a momentary hesitation, Gideon shrugged. "Doesn't matter now, anyway. They broke up years ago. Deborah can hardly stand to hear his name now."

Adrienne wondered if that meant some of the old feelings still burned in Gideon's sister, as she suspected they did in Dylan Smith. Not that it was any of her business, of course, and she could be way off base, but there had been something in Dylan's expression...

Closing the subject about the officer and his sister, Gideon pushed a hand through his hair. "Guess I'll get back to work. Unless you need something?" he added as an afterthought. "Are you hungry or anything?"

"No, I'm fine. But, Gideon, isn't there something useful I can do for you? I came all this way to help you plan the next stage of your writing career, but since you've obviously fallen a little behind, isn't there something I can do to help you catch up? I'm stranded here for a few days, anyway."

He seemed about to refuse her offer, then apparently gave it a second thought. "Actually, you could help. If you're serious, I mean."

"I'm absolutely serious. Tell me what I can do."

"Let's move to my office. You need help getting there?"

"No." She thought it was rather cute the way he offered his assistance so awkwardly and self-consciously, but of course she would never tell him so. *Cute* was probably not a word Gideon would want applied to him.

"I'm getting rather proficient with these things," she said instead, reaching for the crutches.

Gideon's office was the only part of his home that could be described as cluttered. Both his computer desk and the writing desk on the other side of the room were stacked with papers, files and books, and were covered in yellow sticky notes scrawled with cryptic notes to himself. The room's built-in bookcases were filled to overflowing, and extra books were stacked in corners.

A deep metal tray on the writing desk apparently served as his In basket; it was piled so high with what appeared to be unopened mail that the whole stack looked to be in danger of collapsing. Adrienne suspected a couple of unopened certified letters from her were buried in that pile.

Meticulously neat and organized in other areas of his life, Gideon had lost control completely in here. "Help," he said simply.

She didn't need detailed instructions. "Why don't I start with the mail?" she suggested, moving toward the writing desk. "I'll try to separate business correspondence from bills and personal letters."

He looked relieved. "Open everything. There's nothing private in there. I'm sure some of the bills are due, though I try not to get too far behind on those. I don't know what the rest of the stuff is, but most of it can probably go straight to the trash."

His tone effectively erased any hesitation she might have felt about wading into his mail. He sounded almost grateful—for Gideon, at least—that she was willing to do so.

She spent the next hour opening, scanning and separating the mail. She found bills that needed paying immediately, her own letters and a few from his publisher, several you-have-already-been-approved credit card solicitations, requests from charities, two requests for interviews from area newspapers, a couple of invitations to speak at junior-high career days—and a big stack of fan mail that had been forwarded from his publisher.

"You haven't answered any of these?" she asked, flipping through page after page of glowing praise.

Glancing away from the keyboard he'd been pounding the entire time, he shrugged. "I don't know what to say to them. I'm glad they like my books, but I don't know why they're writing to me."

"Just to let you know they enjoy your stories. You brought them pleasure and they wanted to thank you. For heaven's sake, Gideon, these are people who went to the trouble of complimenting you. You should thank them—both as a courtesy and as good public relations practice."

"Maybe you could answer a few of them for me?" he suggested. "You're probably better at that sort of thing than I am."

"I'm your agent, not your secretary."

"You did offer to help. And the more time I spend on that stuff, the later I'll be delivering this book."

She gave him a look. "You're shameless."

"What can I say? I'm drowning here."

She had to give him that. The office *was* a wreck. "Bring me my laptop and I'll see what I can do."

He flashed her one of his sneakily charming smiles— the kind that made her hands clench in her lap beneath the desk. "I'll be right back."

"And bring a diet cola with you, too," she called after him.

If he was going to manipulate her into serving as his secretary, the least he could do was serve her a cold drink.

* * *

Gideon never would have believed that he would be able to concentrate on his work with someone else in the office with him—he hadn't even been able to do so when Isabelle had sat at the other desk quietly coloring pictures. But for some reason Adrienne's presence didn't bother him. Just as he'd been able to work while knowing she was in another room, he had no trouble focusing on his story with her at the other desk.

Actually, he had gotten quite a bit of writing done since she'd arrived, even if she had caused a few inconveniences. But she had helped him with Isabelle, and now she was clearing away some of the stacks of mail that had been nagging at the edges of his consciousness lately.

Yes, he thought smugly, hitting a couple of keys to begin a new chapter, every writer needed a good agent.

It took Adrienne about two hours to reach the bottom of Gideon's In basket. She surveyed her work with satisfaction.

The ads and solicitations had been consigned to the now-overflowing wastebasket. The fan mail had all been answered, the stack of replies printed, waiting for Gideon's approval and signature. Bills were stacked in order of due date; she had already nagged him into writing checks for the most pressing, which she had then stuffed into envelopes and stamped so he could mail them when he fetched Isabelle.

The last item remaining in the metal tray was a battered manila envelope with a San Diego postmark dated several weeks earlier. Inside she found a sealed, letter-size white envelope addressed to Gideon, but not stamped, as if someone had intended to mail it, but had never gotten around to it.

She unfolded the single sheet of paper that had been enclosed with the white envelope. "Gideon?"

He responded without looking away from the computer screen. "Mmm?"

"Here's a letter addressed to you that was found in a box of your father's belongings," she said, summarizing the note she'd just perused. "Apparently, it was in the possession of a Mrs. Barbara Houston, who died recently."

She saw Gideon's shoulders stiffen before he answered. "Just set it aside. I'll get to it later."

"Who was Barbara Houston?"

"Isabelle's mother was Barbara Houston's niece. Isabelle lived with Mrs. Houston after her parents died, until Mrs. Houston became ill and sent Isabelle to Nathan."

Adrienne studied the sealed white envelope, noting that there was no return address. "Do you think this is a letter from your father?"

"Could be." He sounded supremely disinterested.

Adrienne didn't buy his act for a minute. "Don't you want to know what it says?"

"Not particularly. My father died a year ago. There's nothing in that letter that could make any difference now."

She frowned. "That sounds rather cold. What if he wanted to repair things between you? What if he apologized in this letter for whatever it was that went wrong between the two of you? Wouldn't it make you feel better to know that he cared enough to make the effort?"

He turned to face her then, his eyes hard. "Look, Adrienne, you and your father probably have a close relationship, since you work for him, which, I'm sure, makes him very happy. It must be hard for you to understand that not everyone has that type of father-child attachment. Nothing I ever did pleased my father, and there's nothing he could have said in that letter that could make up for the things he did to me or the rest of my family.''

She bit her lip as he turned back to his computer. Looking down at the neat stacks of mail that had given her such satisfaction earlier, she said quietly, ''You're wrong about me not understanding. My relationship with my father isn't at all what you assumed. To be honest, it's very strained and distant. I've never been able to live up to his standards, either, and I've spent twenty-eight years trying.''

Though he didn't look around again, his tone was just a bit warmer when he asked, ''Why do you keep trying?''

''Because my mother died when I was twelve, and he's the only family I have,'' she answered simply. ''He would probably adjust quite well if I severed all ties between us, but I'm not sure I'm prepared to be completely alone.''

Gideon had his mother and his siblings. Whether he professed to be close to them or not, she had already recognized the bond he felt with them. *He* was the one who couldn't understand what it was like to have no one at all.

''I'm hungry,'' she said abruptly, reaching for her crutches. ''I think I'll go make a sandwich. Do you want me to make one for you while I'm at it?''

''No, thanks. I'm not hungry. But why don't you let me make you a sandwich? You don't need to be—''

''Thank you, but I would rather do it myself,'' she interrupted firmly. ''I need the exercise.''

She hobbled out of the room before he could argue further. This time his clumsy attempt at solicitude had failed to charm her.

Chapter Six

Gideon was still thinking about the things Adrienne had let slip when he parked in front of Isabelle's school a short while later. It sounded as though her relationship with her father was as tangled and painful as his had been. If so, she needed to find the courage to cut the cord if she was ever going to be happy.

He'd figured out quite young that he couldn't spend his entire life trying to fulfill someone else's expectations. Shortly after that, he'd learned the hard way that having expectations for anyone else inevitably led to disillusionment and disappointment.

His solution had been to pretty much cut himself off from everyone. He didn't try to please anyone else, and he didn't expect anyone to do otherwise for him. When he was in the mood for company, he found it—no strings, no promises, no expectations. When he wanted to be around family, he had his mother and Nathan nearby, and Deborah, during her infrequent visits home.

Isabelle was a new element in his family mix, but he was adapting to her well enough. He had actually grown quite fond of her, as much as he allowed himself to care for anyone. He could give a hand with her this time without entangling himself in any long-term obligations.

His way was working out very well for him. He didn't describe himself as a happy sort of guy, but he supposed he was content enough. Adrienne could take a few lessons from him, he told himself with a touch of superiority.

Parents who had arrived at the same time as Gideon to collect their offspring nodded greetings to him with a combination of curiosity and wariness when he entered the school. He knew his reputation around town—the reclusive, often surly son of the man who had caused the biggest scandal to hit this area in decades.

Inclined for those reasons not to like him, the locals were still rather impressed that he'd become a noted author. The people of this town didn't want to totally alienate Gideon—just in case he ever became really famous, like John Grisham or some of those other Mississippi celebrities.

He found the situation rather amusing, though he made no effort to play any social games with them. He had yet to accept any invitations to speak to local writers' groups or civic clubs. Anything he had to say, they could find in his books.

Isabelle waited for him in her classroom, her little purple backpack strapped in place, her expression somber. She reached out to take his hand, and he thought she clung to him somewhat more tightly than usual.

"She's been awfully quiet this afternoon," her teacher confided in a stage whisper. "I don't know if she's tired or not feeling well, but you might want to keep an eye on her this evening.''

The possibility that Isabelle could be ill was enough to strike fear into him. What the heck did he know about taking care of a sick kid? He was already dealing with an injured agent.

As Adrienne's rental car had been taken out of commission, he'd brought his truck. The booster seat had been retrieved from the wrecked rental, so he hoisted Isabelle into it and made sure she was safely strapped in before he climbed into the driver's seat and fastened his own seat belt. Only when they were on the road toward his house did he find the nerve to ask the uncharacteristically silent child, ''Aren't you feeling well, Isabelle?''

''I feel okay.''

Her tone was so dispirited that he felt his jaw tense. ''Uh, is something else wrong? Anything you want to talk about?''

''No.'' She looked out the passenger window, and he was suddenly struck by her resemblance to their father.

It wasn't just that she had their father's coloring, though, like Nathan and Deborah, Isabelle was blond, fair-skinned and blue-eyed. Gideon had inherited his mother's brown hair and deep-green eyes, which had always made him feel somewhat like a dark changeling among his fair siblings. At the moment it was Isabelle's expression that reminded him so forcibly of Stuart McCloud—a set, inscrutable mask that effectively concealed anything she might be thinking or feeling. He'd been told he most resembled his father when he unconsciously assumed that same expression. It was particularly disconcerting to recognize it in his four-year-old half sister.

They made the remainder of the drive in silence. Gideon supposed he should try harder to find out what was both-

ering Isabelle, and he might have done so, had he not had
the advantage of knowing Adrienne was waiting for them.
Adrienne would probably know just what to do to find out
what was bothering Isabelle, and then just what to say to
make everything all right again.

Adrienne was as bewildered by Isabelle's behavior as
Gideon had been.

"Something is obviously wrong," she murmured to
Gideon late in the afternoon. "She hasn't said half a dozen
words since she got home from school, and that is just so
unlike her that I can't help but worry."

Frowning in frustration, Gideon pushed a hand through
his hair. "All she wants to do is sit in the den and watch
TV. She didn't even want a snack, though I offered ice
cream, her favorite food."

"She must be coming down with something. Maybe you
should call your mother or your brother."

"And tell them what? That Isabelle's too quiet? No fever, no complaints of pain, no other symptoms of illness,
how are they supposed to know what's wrong? And I can't
expect Mom to leave her sister, or Nathan to cut his honeymoon short, just because Isabelle's unusually subdued."

"Then maybe your other sister?"

He snorted. "Deborah has spent even less time around
Isabelle than I have. She's still coming to terms with having another sibling in the family."

Whatever their father had done to the family, Adrienne
couldn't imagine anyone holding it against sweet little Isabelle. But it seemed that she and Gideon were on their
own with this dilemma, whatever its cause.

She drew a breath and nodded. "I'll go try to talk to
her again."

"We'll both try again." He followed close behind her

as she limped into the den, deliberately leaving the cumbersome crutches behind.

Isabelle was still parked in front of the TV, her eyes focused almost unblinkingly on the screen. Yet she seemed to find little pleasure in the taped shenanigans. Adrienne settled on the couch beside the child while Gideon took one of the chairs.

"What would you like for dinner tonight, Isabelle?" Adrienne asked, hoping an innocuous opening would lead to a more meaningful conversation.

Without looking away from the television, Isabelle shrugged. "Doesn't matter."

Adrienne looked at Gideon. *Your turn.*

He cleared his throat, then snapped his fingers. "This is Wednesday. Didn't your schedule say you have a dance class at five?"

Isabelle scooted a couple of inches closer to Adrienne and looked at Gideon with big, somber eyes. "Do I have to go? I don't want to."

"You want to miss your dance class?" Adrienne asked her. "Dance class is fun, isn't it? I know I always enjoyed going to them when I was your age."

Gideon raised an eyebrow, as if he were picturing her in a tutu, but she kept her attention focused on Isabelle. "I'll go with you, if you like."

Isabelle shook her head. "I don't want to go."

Adrienne and Gideon looked at each other again, and he obviously had no more idea what to do than she did. After a moment he shrugged. "Okay, no dance class tonight. If she's coming down with something, she doesn't need to be spreading it around to the other kids."

She had to concede that he'd made a point. "Okay. So, what would you like to do, Isabelle? Do you want me to play a game with you?"

Isabelle shook her head. "Not right now," she said, then crawled without warning into Adrienne's lap. She nestled her head in Adrienne's throat and gave a little sigh. "Could I just sit here for a little while?"

Nonplussed, she felt Isabelle's face with her hand again, but the soft cheeks were cool, without even a hint of fever. "Sweetheart, are you sure nothing hurts? No tummy ache or sore throat or ear ache or anything?"

Isabelle shook her head against Adrienne's shoulder. "I don't hurt anywhere."

Settling more comfortably back into the cushions, Adrienne wrapped her arms around the child and prepared to stay that way for a while. Sometimes it was easy to forget that Isabelle was so very young, little more than a baby. And here she was stuck with two rather clueless caretakers who were practically strangers to her, even if one of them was her brother. It was entirely possible that she was simply homesick and needed a little cuddling.

Gideon stood and pushed his hands into the pockets of his jeans. "It's a little early, but I guess I'll go start dinner. Any special requests?"

Adrienne shook her head. "Anything's fine with us, isn't is, Isabelle?"

Isabelle nodded. "Gideon's a good cook."

Gideon looked a bit startled and then, to Adrienne's amusement, rather pleased by the compliment. "Yes," she murmured, "Gideon is a very good cook."

With typically masculine embarrassment, Gideon muttered something incomprehensible and made his escape, leaving Adrienne rocking Isabelle soothingly as they watched cartoons together.

Gideon spent quite a while preparing dinner—teriyaki chicken with rice and vegetables. For dessert, he made brownies from a mix he found in the pantry. He told himself the reason for the special meal was to tempt Isabelle into eating, certainly not to show off his culinary skills.

He was just putting the finishing touches on the meal when the telephone rang. He glared at it for a moment, then gave in and reached for the receiver. If this was a telemarketer, he wouldn't be responsible for his actions.

But the caller was his sister, Deborah. "You answered the phone," she said in exaggerated astonishment. "Wow."

"Since you call me fairly frequently and get through, you needn't act so surprised. What's up, Deb?"

"If you think a call every couple of months or so is frequent..." She let the sentence trail off, then went on, "Actually, I'm trying to reach mother. I've been calling her since last night and I keep getting her machine. Do you know if anything's wrong?"

Succinctly explaining the situation with their aunt, Gideon added, "I'm surprised she didn't let you know."

"I've been out of town on a business trip. She left a message on my machine that Aunt Wanda had been hurt, but she sounded rushed and didn't give many details."

"She's been staying at the hospital with Wanda."

"Surely she doesn't have Isabelle with her."

"No, actually, I have Isabelle."

"You?" Deborah seemed to doubt that she had heard him correctly. "You're baby-sitting?"

"Yes. It wasn't as if Mom gave me any other choice."

"I'm just surprised that even Mom's tactics got you to agree to this. What did she use? Guilt? Pleas? Threats?"

"A combination of inducements, actually," Gideon answered dryly.

"So, how's it going? Have you learned how to do a French braid yet? Sing a lullaby?"

"I've been getting by," he said, feeling just a touch defensive. And then—because he knew she would find out eventually—he felt compelled to add, "I've had a little help. My agent is staying here for a few days. She and Isabelle have sort of bonded."

He glanced toward the kitchen doorway, picturing Adrienne in the other room with Isabelle snuggled in her arms. As he had stood there looking at them, he'd been aware of mixed emotions—one of them an inappropriate touch of envy. He wouldn't have minded having Adrienne's arms around him.

It wasn't the first time he'd acknowledged his attraction to her, but he was just starting to realize how strong that attraction had grown. Which didn't mean there were any more-dangerous emotions involved, of course. Sure, he wanted to hit the sheets with her, but he was still fully prepared for her to leave in a day or two and go back to being an efficiently professional voice on the other end of the telephone line.

Not that he was ready for her to leave just yet, but only because he still needed her help with Isabelle, he assured himself.

"What's your agent doing there?"

"She came to discuss some publishing offers and to map out some career plans with me." Not that they had actually accomplished either of those things, he added to himself.

All things considered, she had been remarkably patient with him. Not only had he avoided talking business with her since she'd arrived, but he'd closed himself in his office for hours at a time, manipulated her into helping out with his little sister, which had indirectly resulted in her being injured, and he'd even dumped secretarial duties onto her. And still she was doing everything she could to assist him with Isabelle and his writing.

Was it any wonder he suspected he might miss her—a little—when she returned to New York?

"*You* could always come give me a hand," he suggested to his sister.

"No way. I don't do kids, remember? If the rest of you want to clutter things up with the result of Dad's thoughtlessness, that's your choice, but I have a life."

Deborah sounded cold and cynical—as Gideon himself had been accused of being on many occasions—but he knew that with Deborah, it was all facade. She'd erected it so successfully that it probably fooled most people—but Gideon knew her better. His own resistance to forming emotional bonds was based on selfish convenience—or so he'd always told himself. Deborah's was founded on fear.

"I'll tell Mom to call you next time she checks in."

"Okay, thanks. Good luck with everything there."

"I'll give your best to Isabelle."

"Yeah." Her voice was almost brittle now. "You do that."

Hanging up the phone, Gideon turned back to his dinner preparations. He understood Deborah's bitterness, of course—far too well—but he was beginning to think she was missing out by not giving herself a chance to get to know Isabelle better. As resistant as he'd been, himself, to letting another sibling into his life at this late stage, he'd grown fond of his little sister. He just hoped this newest problem wouldn't prove to be a total catastrophe.

Adrienne was relieved that Isabelle seemed to perk up a bit during the excellent dinner Gideon had prepared for them. Though Isabelle only picked at the food at first, she seemed to quickly decide that she liked it. She ate enough to satisfy Adrienne and Gideon, then finished the meal with a small brownie and another half glass of milk.

"That was really good, Gideon," she said when she'd finished.

Her brother set his tea glass on the table. "Glad you liked it."

"You're a better cook than Nate. He mostly opens cans or orders out. Mrs. T.'s a good cook, though."

"Mrs. T. is Nathan's housekeeper, Fayrene Tuckerman," Gideon said for Adrienne's benefit.

She could tell he was amused by Isabelle's comparison of his cooking to his brother's. "Does your brother's new wife cook?" she asked Isabelle.

The child frowned. "I don't know. Mrs. T. cooks for all of us."

Once again Gideon elucidated. "Caitlin is Nathan's law partner. They're both fine lawyers, but domestic chores aren't high on their priority lists."

Unlike Gideon, Adrienne mused. She had already figured out that he did all his own housework. He was much too independent to rely on anyone for his needs—not even a housekeeper.

She wondered for a moment if a couple of busy lawyers had time to be good guardians for Isabelle, but she remembered that Gideon had said the three of them adored each other. Isabelle certainly seemed attached to her oldest brother and his new wife.

It was silly of Adrienne to suddenly feel a bit proprietary toward the child. Protective. Of all the adults involved in Isabelle's life, she had the *least* right to question any arrangements for Isabelle's care.

Encouraged by the little girl's improving mood, Adrienne asked what was planned for preschool the next day. Keeping her eyes on her brownie, Isabelle replied quietly, "I'm not going to school tomorrow."

Glancing at Gideon, Adrienne raised her eyebrows. "You're not?"

"No. I don't want to."

Apparently, she had stumbled onto a clue to Isabelle's odd behavior. "Did something happen at school today?"

Isabelle shrugged.

Adrienne tried again. "Did your teacher say something to upset you? Or one of your classmates?"

Isabelle's lower lip poked out. "I don't want to talk about school."

Adrienne backed off. She didn't know how to push any harder without further upsetting Isabelle. Maybe Gideon could get more out of her.

But Gideon had no more luck than Adrienne had. Just questioning Isabelle about school set off pouts and, eventually, tears. The first teardrop caused Gideon to retreat, leaving Adrienne to soothe the child, dry her eyes and take her off to bathe her, tuck her into bed and read her a soothingly silly bedtime story.

Only when she was sure Isabelle was asleep did Adrienne rejoin Gideon in the den, where she found him pacing and running his hands through his already disordered hair.

"You need to get off that foot," he said curtly when she entered. "You're limping badly. Are you in pain?"

"It's not too bad," she said, then sank gratefully onto the couch. Her leg was throbbing all the way to her hip, though she had no intention of saying so. Gideon had enough to worry about.

He resumed his pacing. "What do you suppose happened at school today?"

"Probably she got into a squabble with another child. That's fairly common in preschool, I think. It will blow over."

"And in the meantime? Do I make her go to school tomorrow even if she's kicking and screaming in protest?"

Adrienne spread her hands. "I don't know. I don't suppose it would hurt her to miss a day of preschool, but that wouldn't solve her problems, either."

"I'm not sure I can make her go if she cries and pleads."

Adrienne nodded in empathy. "I'm not sure I could, either. Maybe we should just play it by ear. Maybe by morning she'll have forgotten all about it."

"I hope you're right." He paused a moment, then asked, "How about some tea?"

"Yes, thank you. And make a cup for yourself. We could both use something warm and soothing."

He hesitated a moment, then nodded and left the room without saying anything else.

Adrienne sat looking after him, her lower lip caught between her teeth. Every once in a while an expression crossed Gideon's face that made her wonder just what was going on in his mind. Was she completely misguided or was he attracted to her—at least superficially? And if he was, how did she feel about that?

It was true that her feelings about him had undergone several changes in the past three days. Initially expecting to find a grumpy, eccentric middle-aged man, she had discovered instead that he was a grumpy, eccentric—and drop-dead gorgeous—young man, filled with contradictions.

At first he had seemed cold and unfriendly, as he could be when he wanted to be, but his connection to his family was strong. Yet he wouldn't even open the last letter his father had written to him. He seemed indifferent about advancing his career, but he worked very hard at his craft. She had watched him write earlier, and she had realized that he invested everything in his words. It wasn't that he especially enjoyed the process; more, it was something as vital to him as breathing.

He fascinated her. And, yes, she was attracted to him. Extremely attracted, actually. Every time their eyes met, her breath lodged in her throat. And every time he touched her, even by accident, her knees went weak.

So what was she going to do about it? Ignore her feelings? Deny them? She certainly couldn't act on them, not and maintain a professional relationship with her client.

He returned bearing two steaming mugs. "I took your advice. Made a cup for myself."

She smiled and accepted her cup from him. She was rather surprised when he sat on the couch beside her rather than returning to the chair in which he'd sat earlier.

He leaned back into the cushions with a soft sigh. "This baby-sitting gig is wearing me out. I don't know how Nathan adjusted to it so easily."

"What's Nathan like? Is he like you?"

"Hardly. Nathan's the life of the party, whereas I'm the classic wet blanket sitting in a corner and scowling. Nathan's an almost compulsive caretaker, always the responsible, concerned older brother, the dutiful son. Even to the father who didn't deserve his loyalty."

"Except for the party thing, you don't sound all that different to me. Haven't you spent the past week taking care of your sister as a favor to your mother?"

That made him frown. "I'm not really like Nathan at all. You simply found me under highly unusual circumstances."

Rather than argue with him, she sipped her tea.

"So when do you have to go back to New York?" Gideon asked after a minute. "Are you missing any important meetings or appointments?"

"Actually, this is the first week of a two-week vacation. I'm not missing anything."

He set his barely touched mug on the table and turned to face her. "You came here to talk business with me on your vacation?"

She shrugged. "It was the only time I had available."

"Lousy vacation."

She laughed softly at that and set her mug beside his. "It hasn't been so bad."

"Are you kidding? You've spent the past few days helping me with my sister and my mail, hurting your ankle—and now dealing with Isabelle's emotional breakdown."

She smoothed a hand over her black slacks. "It really hasn't been that bad. I've enjoyed being with Isabelle and, well…"

"Have you enjoyed being with *me?*"

Something in his voice made her look at him suspiciously. Was that a glint of teasing in his eyes? It seemed unlike Gideon, but then, what did she know? She'd met him for the first time only forty-eight hours ago.

"Being with you has been…interesting."

"I'm not sure how to take that."

She laced her fingers in her lap. "Let's just say I'm glad I finally had a chance to meet my client—and my favorite writer. I adore your books."

For the first time, she saw Gideon look almost flustered. "Yeah?"

She couldn't help but smile. "Does that really surprise you so much? I've told you before that I like your books, when we've spoken over the phone."

"Well, yeah…but you never said it quite like that."

"Like what?"

"Like a reader, rather than my agent."

She laughed softly. "I *am* a reader. I couldn't do my job well if I didn't love books."

"No, I suppose not."

"With a little more push in the public relations area, you'd really take off. I think you're well on your way to becoming the next Dean Koontz or Michael Crichton."

"I'm not trying to become the next anybody. I just write what I want."

"I know. But there's more to an author's life than just writing, you know. There are interviews and book signings, your picture on book jackets—"

"What's wrong with just writing a damned good book?"

"Nothing. In fact, that's the most important thing you can do to advance your career. But—"

"But nothing. I'm not good with people, you know that. Put me on TV or at one of those boring book signings, and I'd probably torpedo my own career by alienating the readers I already have."

"You would be fine," she assured him. "You just need some prepping. I'd like to sign you up with a good public relations firm."

"I'd rather have my toenails rotated."

Shaking her head, she said, "We'll talk about it tomorrow. That will give you time to think about my suggestions."

"Won't make me like them any more," he muttered.

She shook her head. "I think you're the only client I have who doesn't want to get rich and famous."

"I don't mind the rich part," he admitted with a wry smile. "It's the fame I have trouble with."

"I'm sure you'll find a way to come to terms with it—especially if it means you can keep doing what you enjoy."

"Mmm." He propped an elbow on the back of the couch and studied her. "So what would you be doing with your vacation time if you weren't here baby-sitting Isabelle and me?"

Had he inched a bit closer or was it her imagination? There was nothing apparent in his expression except a mild interest in her answer. Since she couldn't think of a way to scoot away without calling attention to her action, she gripped her fingers more tightly in her lap and concentrated on the question. "I didn't have any specific plans. It's the first time I've taken off in quite a while, so I thought I would just relax, do some reading and shopping, maybe watch a few of the movies I've missed lately. And I had tentatively planned to spend a couple of days in Boston next week visiting an old friend."

His expression didn't change. "Old boyfriend?"

"Girlfriend," she corrected. "College roommate."

"Ah. So is there a boyfriend in New York?"

She thought of the man she had dated infrequently during the past year, a stockbroker who had recently begun to hint about marriage, mostly because it was time for that step in his longtime life plan. He had considered her a suitable mate, one who came very close to matching his "profile" of the type of woman he wanted as his wife and the mother of his children.

Though she liked Robert, his approach to marriage had seemed too calculated. While he had spoken of affection and loyalty and commitment, he had never used the words "love" or "passion." A couple of her friends had questioned her sanity when she'd begun to extricate herself from the relationship—after all, decent, successful men who were interested in marriage were hard to find. But she simply couldn't get excited about being married because she fit some preexisting, arbitrary profile.

"No," she said. "There's no boyfriend."

His elbow still resting on the back of the couch, he turned sideways so he could see her better, propping his cheek on his fist. "Do you enjoy your work?"

"It pays the bills."

"Not exactly a glowing endorsement."

She smiled and shrugged. "I'm good at my job, and I find it interesting most of the time. It's quite demanding, of course—long hours on the phone and in meetings, confrontations with editors on behalf of my authors, stacks of reading, attending the occasional writers' conference. But most jobs are challenging—that's why they call it work, right?"

"Did your father pressure you to join his firm?"

She stared down at her hands. "It was what he always wanted. Not because he wanted to spend that much time with me, but because he liked the idea of having someone he could control as his second in command."

"He controls you?"

"Like one of those radio-operated airplanes," she said dryly. "Do you suppose we could talk about something else now?"

"Of course." He reached over to brush a strand of hair from her cheek. "How's your ankle?"

His touch caused a tiny shiver to course through her. Her voice was just a bit hoarse when she said, "It's better, thanks."

"It's swollen again. You've been standing on it too long today. I'm sure it hurts like hell, but you're not a complainer, are you?"

"I try not to be." Whining and complaining had never been tolerated by her father; she'd learned early to keep her troubles to herself.

His mouth twisted wryly. "When I hurt, everyone

knows about it. I've been told I'm a rather...difficult patient.''

That made her laugh. ''I'd just bet you are.''

His gaze lingered on her mouth, and her smile wavered. Was he suddenly leaning closer? She cleared her throat. ''Maybe I should...''

What? She couldn't think of one reasonable excuse to retreat, except, of course, cowardice.

He was definitely moving closer, and there was a gleam in his eyes now that made her pulse speed up. ''Um, Gideon...''

''You know all those times we talked on the phone during the past couple of years?''

''Yes?''

His fingers slid down the curve of her jaw. ''I didn't picture you looking quite like this.''

''What—'' She started again. ''What did you think I looked like?''

''Different.'' His fingertips traced her cheek, and then the pad of his thumb moved lightly across her lower lip. It was as if he were a blind man learning her face by feel alone, and the sensation was decidedly erotic. It wasn't hard to imagine him exploring the rest of her body the same way.

It wasn't hard to picture herself learning *his* body the same way. And that image was so tempting that she knew she had to move *now,* before she did something really foolish and unprofessional—like make a pass at her client.

''I think I'll read for a while before I turn in,'' she said, scooting away from him. ''I have a couple of manuscripts to look over, one that looks pretty good, another that has so many flaws I'm not sure it's fixable. But I thought I would look at it one more time, just to make sure I'm being fair before returning it to the author. I can't wait to read your new book when you finish it, by the way. I'm really looking forward to it."

He studied her face for a moment, his gaze so intense that she wondered if he saw too much there, but then he asked, "How would you like to read it now?"

"It's finished?"

"No. But I've printed out what I've written to this point. Sometimes I edit more efficiently on paper than on screen."

"I thought you had a policy of not letting anyone read your work before it's finished. You don't even like to submit sample chapters to your editor."

"Not usually, no. But I've had some problems with this one, and you've always given me good advice in the past."

Those words delighted her as much as her compliments about his books had seemed to please him earlier. "I would love to read your manuscript."

He nodded, though he looked as though he half regretted the offer. "Be sure and tell me if there's anything about it that bothers you. I can't promise to be gracious about taking the criticism—I never am—but I want you to be honest, anyway."

"I'm always honest with my clients," she said firmly.

He seemed rather amused by the fervency of her assurance. "Go on back and put your feet up, and I'll bring the manuscript to you."

"In the bedroom, you mean?"

His eyes met hers. "Yes."

"Oh. Well, you can just bring it in here and I'll—"

"You need to get that foot elevated. It wouldn't hurt to ice it for a few minutes, since it's swelling again."

"I'll take an anti-inflammatory."

He shrugged. "Whatever you think best."

Pushing herself to her feet, she limped awkwardly toward the doorway. "I'll wait for you in the bedroom."

There was an undercurrent of laughter in his voice when he called after her, "That sounds good to me."

She discovered then that she could move more quickly than she'd realized while hopping on one foot.

Chapter Seven

Though Gideon tended to be a restless sleeper on the best of nights, rarely needing more than five or six hours total, he slept very little that night. The couch in the office was perfectly comfortable. He'd spent many nights on it after writing until the wee hours and finally collapsing into sleep. So it wasn't physical discomfort that caused him to prowl the dark hallways during those long hours.

He was concerned that Isabelle was getting sick or had encountered problems at school that he was unprepared to deal with. He certainly didn't relish the prospect of a parent-teacher conference with him in the role of parent. But it wasn't Isabelle's odd behavior that had kept him awake—not entirely, anyway.

His mind filled with images of Adrienne, lying asleep in his bed. She would look flushed and warm and tousled, as she had when her soft moans of pain had led him to her. Something else was drawing him to her now and it was all he could do to resist.

She'd still been fully dressed when he had taken his unfinished manuscript to her. Sitting on his bed, her back propped against the pillows, her swollen foot stretched in front of her, she had looked both fetching and self-conscious. Attractive enough to make his palms sweat yet vulnerable in a way that made him keep his distance.

He'd been strung tight as a banjo string ever since. Partly because it made him nervous letting someone else read his work in progress—something he almost never trusted to anyone. But mostly because he had left that room with a need so deep he ached from it.

Maybe it was time for Adrienne to go back to New York, Isabelle notwithstanding.

If Adrienne had been under the illusion that Isabelle never misbehaved, she learned differently Thursday morning. She and Gideon were treated to an outburst that came perilously close to a tantrum when they tried to get Isabelle ready for school.

"I don't *want* to go to school!" she cried out, stamping one foot, her face red and tear-streaked. "I want to stay here!"

Leaving her sobbing in the den, her face buried against her stuffed owl, Adrienne and Gideon retreated to the kitchen for a hasty conference.

"We'll let her stay home," Gideon decided, looking shaken by the flare-up. "Everyone needs an occasional mental health day."

Adrienne tended to agree with him, mostly out of fear of what they might encounter if they insisted Isabelle go to school. And yet, "What if she refuses to go again tomorrow?"

"A four-year-old dropout." Gideon squeezed the back of his neck with one hand. "Maybe we can get her a job serving Happy Meals."

"This isn't funny, Gideon."

"No," he admitted. "But we might as well lighten up about it. Mom or Nathan will be home soon, and they'll probably know a heck of a lot better than we do how to handle this. I agreed to baby-sit for a few days, but I never promised to handle emotional crises."

Adrienne bit her lip, hoping they were doing the right thing by giving in to the child's tantrum. Adrienne knew her father would never have tolerated such behavior. But she also remembered how she had so often longed for him to listen to her problems and offer sympathy rather than lectures.

"You had better call the school and tell them Isabelle won't be there today," she advised him. "They'll worry if you don't."

He didn't look enthusiastic about making the call. "Miss Thelma will probably remind me of my total incompetence as a baby-sitter and ask me again what my mother was thinking leaving a helpless child in my care."

"Maybe you should ask *her* what's going on at her school that's making Isabelle almost hysterical at the prospect of going back," Adrienne suggested in return. "She's perfectly happy here, but there's something at school that's upsetting her badly."

Gideon nodded. "Maybe I will ask her that."

"I'll go sit with Isabelle while you make the call."

"See if you can get her to stop crying, will you? I can't handle much more of that."

"I'll do my best."

It took bribery to stop the flood. Adrienne wasn't proud

of herself, but she was desperate. "Please tell me what you want, Isabelle."

The child sniffled. "I don't want to go to school."

"I've already told you, you don't have to go today."

Her lips quivered. "I want Nate and Caitlin to come home."

Homesickness. Just as Adrienne had suspected. It wasn't the full explanation, of course, but it was part of the problem. "Your brother will be home soon. Maybe you can talk to him on the phone later, okay?"

"Okay." Isabelle rested her cheek on Hedwig's fuzzy head, looking so miserable that Adrienne's heart twisted.

This was more than a tantrum, she decided abruptly. More than a childish power play. This child was hurting badly.

Her original thought had been to suggest they make no effort to entertain Isabelle. Hours of boredom might make preschool look pretty good, no matter what difficulties she had encountered there.

Now Adrienne's thinking had changed. If she could get Isabelle to relax, maybe she would admit in an unguarded moment what had upset her so badly. "What would you like to do today? Surely there's something you can think of that might be fun."

Isabelle sniffed again and shook her head. "I don't know."

"There's a new Disney film, isn't there? Have you seen it yet?"

A flicker of interest crossed the child's damp face. "No, not yet."

"Would you like to see it this afternoon?"

She swiped the back of one hand across her cheek. "Okay."

Adrienne pulled a tissue out of her pocket and handed

it over. "Wipe your face and blow your nose and I'll talk to Gideon about our plans, all right? You want to go play with your toys or something for a little while?"

Isabelle hesitated. "Gideon won't make me go to school?"

"No, not today. But maybe we can talk about school again later?"

"I hate school. I don't ever want to go back." Isabelle stomped her little foot for emphasis, then ran out of the room.

Rubbing her aching temples, Adrienne wondered what could possibly have happened to turn a happy, sweet-natured, enthusiastic little student into a sullen, rebellious wannabe dropout.

And then she wondered if she and Gideon were up to the challenge of changing her back.

Gideon had no interest in attending the Disney movie. Claiming that he needed to work, he offered to drive them to the mall where the matinee was playing. When the film ended, Adrienne and Isabelle could go into the mall's ice-cream shop for a treat, and he would pick them up there, he suggested.

Adrienne thought it sounded like a good plan, with one addition. She asked him to give her an extra half hour or so after the movie, to give her a chance to buy a couple of new tops. She was really getting tired of the few outfits she'd brought with her, she added ruefully. Though he warned her not to put too much strain on her injured ankle, Gideon approved the agenda.

Adrienne was initially concerned that Isabelle would be disappointed her brother wasn't joining them for the movie, but she seemed satisfied with the prospect of a girls-only outing. With typical childhood resilience, her mood had transformed from sullen and tearful to sunny and cheerful, but Adrienne sensed that one reminder of school could trigger another crisis.

Because she didn't want to take that risk, she carefully avoided mentioning anything sensitive. Cowardly, perhaps, but all in all, it seemed much safer.

Pulling up in front of the cinema entrance outside the mall, Gideon shook his head at the sight of the stream of mothers and toddlers going in. "You're sure you want to do this?" he asked Adrienne.

She glanced at Isabelle, who sat between them on the truck seat, looking excited for the first time since she'd come home from school yesterday. "I'm sure."

"You'll be okay on that ankle?"

"I'll be fine." Wrinkling her nose, Adrienne looked down at her bound ankle. She couldn't get her loafer on over the swelling, so she wore a black sock over her bare toes beneath the brace, and her regular shoe on her left foot. She thought it looked ridiculous, but she supposed it would suffice for a Disney matinee.

Gideon assisted her out of the truck, then turned to swing Isabelle out. "So I'll meet the two of you at the ice-cream parlor, right?"

Balancing on the crutches he had insisted she use for the outing, Adrienne nodded. "We'll see you then."

Isabelle tugged at Gideon's shirt. "I'm sorry you have to work and can't see the movie with us, Gideon."

"Maybe some other time," he replied, patting her head. "You have fun with Miss Corley, okay?"

"Okay. I'll take good care of her," she added, looking meaningfully toward the crutches.

Gideon chuckled. "You do that."

Standing on the walkway that led to the ticket window, Adrienne watched as he climbed back into his truck with an easy, masculine grace that made her mouth go dry. She was still watching when he drove out of the parking lot.

"Miss Corley? Aren't we going in?"

Roused by Isabelle's prodding, Adrienne turned toward the ticket window. "Of course we're going in. We'll have a lovely time."

But something told her she would spend the next couple hours thinking of Gideon rather than the animated feature on the movie screen.

As Gideon had wanted for the past week, he returned to a completely empty house. He noticed the silence as soon as he walked in, which was odd, since Adrienne and Isabelle really didn't make that much noise.

Moving straight to his office, he settled in front of his computer and set a timer he kept on his desk for occasions when he dove into his work and worried about time slipping away from him. It wouldn't be entirely uncharacteristic for him to concentrate so fiercely on his writing that five or six hours would slip away before he knew it.

That would not have been the case today.

Just as having someone in his house had interfered with his concentration a few days earlier, now the emptiness seemed to press in on him. It kept drawing him out of his story, making him look at the clock to see if it was time to leave for the mall.

It seemed he always had an excuse not to write these days. He was beginning to wonder if there was more going on here. Was the book so flawed that subconsciously he was *trying* to sabotage it? He didn't know how far Adrienne had gotten last night; Isabelle had kept them so busy today they hadn't had a chance to discuss work.

Pounding his fist against his knee, he gave a low growl of frustration. What the hell was wrong with this book?

Everything had been going smoothly, right on schedule, for the first three hundred pages, and then he'd seemed to crash facefirst into some sort of creative brick wall. He'd written some sixty pages since, but he still wasn't completely satisfied with them. He hated to think he'd have to struggle this hard with the final hundred pages, and, at this rate, heaven only knew when he would get the damned thing finished.

Maybe once Adrienne assured him there was nothing wrong with the story to the point he'd printed out so far, he would be able to proceed more confidently.

He forced himself to wait until the last minute to leave for town. Adrienne and Isabelle were probably enjoying their time together, and he didn't want to appear too eager to be reunited with them. He saved his file—he'd written all of three pages and they weren't very good—and headed for the door, moving a bit too quickly for a man who was reluctant to have his treasured privacy invaded again.

The ice cream parlor was fairly crowded for a Thursday afternoon, but Gideon quickly spotted Adrienne and Isabelle. They sat at a tiny round table flanked by four prissy little chairs, and both of them were smiling.

At Officer Dylan Smith.

"What is it with you, Smith?" he demanded in exasperation, planting his fists on his hips as he loomed beside the table. "Every time I turn around these days, I find you there."

Obviously off-duty, dressed in jeans and a gray-checked cotton shirt worn unbuttoned over a gray T-shirt, Dylan lounged in one of the little chairs with the ease of a man who felt entirely assured of his welcome. His gray eyes gleamed with his usual mocking humor when he looked up at Gideon. "You're just lucky, I guess. Or I am, to keep running into these two lovely ladies."

Isabelle giggled. "Officer Smith likes ice cream as much as I do, Gideon. His favorite flavor is butter pecan and I told him I don't like it, but he said that's okay, it's still his favorite."

She was talking again, at least. Too bad it was about Dylan.

Adrienne motioned him toward the empty chair. "Join us, Gideon. Would you like some ice cream?"

"No." After a momentary hesitation, he dropped into the chair. What else could he do, just stand there watching the three of them eat ice cream and admire each other? Crossing his arms over his chest, he glared at Dylan, all too aware that the four of them were a subject of interest for quite a few of the other patrons.

Adrienne looked at him in exasperation. "Loosen up, will you?" she admonished him quietly. "We've been having a very nice visit."

"Until I came along to ruin it, you mean?"

"I didn't say that."

"The movie was good, Gideon," Isabelle told him, her face beaming behind several smudges of chocolate ice cream. "You should have seen it."

Studying her smile, he decided the outing had done wonders for her. Adrienne's idea had obviously been a good one. Maybe now she would forget whatever toddler grievance had upset her yesterday, and she would be content to return to school tomorrow. "I'm glad you enjoyed it."

"Dylan was just telling us about the big St. Patrick's Day festival this weekend," Adrienne said brightly. "It sounds like a lot of fun."

He shrugged. "I've never been."

"Never?" She looked surprised. "Dylan made it sound as if the whole town turns out for this."

"I've always thought it was ridiculous that a bunch of non-Irish folks from southern Mississippi get together every year to wear green and act like morons."

"Gideon's never been known as a fun sort of guy," Dylan remarked with a smirk that went straight to Gideon's temper.

"Gideon is too fun," Isabelle protested. "He, um, he writes good stories."

Isabelle had never read his stories, of course. She didn't even know what they were about. Though he hadn't done a thing all week to entertain her, she was defending him, anyway, seizing on the first evidence that popped into her mind that he possessed a sense of fun.

Her defiant little gesture touched him, and because it did, he didn't know what to say except, "Thanks, kiddo."

"I stand corrected," Dylan murmured with a smile for Isabelle.

As much as he disliked Dylan for the history between them, Gideon was confident that the other man would take no more chances of upsetting the child.

A neighbor of his mother's, Lucille Mayo, entered the ice cream parlor with two grandchildren in tow. Looking both surprised and avidly curious, she paused by their table.

"Hello, Gideon. And Officer Smith. Nice to see you both." She left unspoken her surprise at seeing them together. Few longtime residents of this town were unaware of the old acrimony between Dylan and the McCloud siblings.

Dylan responded first. "'Afternoon, Mrs. Mayo. You're looking well."

The guy had a real talent for instantly transforming into the smooth-talking charmer, Gideon mused. He had so many faces that it was impossible to know which one was real. These days Dylan was the consummate peace officer—polite, hardworking and by all accounts completely above reproach. But Gideon remembered the angry rebel Dylan had once been. The teenager with a flash-point temper and ready fists.

Gideon clearly recalled the feel of those fists against his own face. Just as he knew how it felt to bruise his knuckles against Dylan's rock-hard jaw.

Lucille turned to him then. "I haven't seen you in a while, Gideon. Are you still writing?"

It was invariably one of the first things people asked him. Because he had quickly grown tired of hearing it, he was often tempted to answer facetiously, something along the line of, "No, I became too successful, so I quit."

Instead, he answered as he always did, with a simple, "Yes."

"How many books have you written now?"

"I'm working on my fifth," he replied somewhat woodenly, dreading the next question. Maybe she wouldn't ask it....

But she did. "Where *do* you get all your ideas?"

Another frequently asked question that seemed to have no sensible reply. Did people think there was a retail store that specialized in story ideas? He pictured a sign printed with the words "This Week's Special: Science Fiction Premises."

He tried to keep his thoughts hidden when he replied, "That's just what I do, Lucille."

"You know I teach ninth-grade English. I wish you would agree to speak to my classes sometime. I know my students would be fascinated by the book-publishing process."

"I doubt they would be fascinated by any talk I would give. As I've told you before, I'm not much of a speaker."

And he would rather jab sharp sticks under his fingernails than face a roomful of ninth-graders, he added silently.

She must have anticipated his response, because she looked more resigned than disappointed. She glanced at Adrienne. "I heard your agent is visiting you. Is this...?"

Gideon nodded, wishing the woman would take her increasingly restless grandchildren and move on. For Adrienne and Isabelle's sake, he tried to sound reasonably polite when he said, "Adrienne Corley, this is my mother's friend, Lucille Mayo. And, Lucille, you know my sister, Isabelle."

The words still sounded a bit strange to him, since he'd only introduced Isabelle as his sister a couple of times, but, oddly enough, they were beginning to feel more natural.

"Yes, of course. It's good to see you again, Isabelle. And it's very nice to meet you, Ms. Corley. You're, um, staying with Gideon this week?"

Gideon felt his eyebrows draw downward into a frown. Lucille had been known to indulge in gossip, and he did not want Adrienne to be the subject of idle speculation. It wasn't that gossip bothered him personally, since he never cared what anyone else said or thought about him, but he saw no reason for his agent to be embarrassed just because she had tried to help him out for a few days.

He should have known Adrienne was quite capable of looking out for herself. The smile she directed toward the older woman was friendly, direct and self-assured. "Yes, I am. Gideon and Isabelle have been gracious enough to let me stay with them while I recuperate from a fall I took earlier this week. I'm going to try to get out of their way as soon as I can get around more easily."

She motioned ruefully toward the crutches propped beside her chair as she spoke, which also drew attention to her bandaged ankle. The message was clear: she considered herself an imposition on him, rather than an invited guest. From her tone, he was merely tolerating her presence and not particularly enjoying it. By mentioning Isabelle, she reminded Lucille that she and Gideon weren't quite alone in his house.

It certainly didn't sound as though they were engaging in a heated fling during her time here.

Her suspicions allayed, Lucille returned the smile. "You poor thing. To come here for a business trip and then to be detained by an injury. It must be very inconvenient for you, being a busy New York agent and all."

"I'm afraid I am falling a bit behind," Adrienne agreed, managing to look politely anxious to be on her way back to New York. "But I am grateful to Gideon for giving me a hand, even when he's so very busy with his own work."

Once again Lucille looked at Gideon in surprise, and he knew it was because of his reputation for being reclusive and inhospitable. Now he would have to painstakingly rebuild that reputation. He wouldn't want the locals to think of him as a soft touch.

"Grandma, we want some ice cream," Lucille's grandson finally piped up, eyeing Isabelle's nearly empty dish with envy. "Please?"

"All right, Justin, I'm coming. Have you heard from your mother, Gideon?"

"She called this morning."

"How's her poor sister?

"She's improving. She may be released from the hospital tomorrow, though she'll still need someone to take care of her for a while."

"You tell Lenore to call me if she needs anything, you hear?"

"I will. And, uh, thank you," he added belatedly.

"She certainly left with a lot to think about, didn't she?" Dylan's smile was sharp-edged again when he glanced at Gideon. "The two of us sitting here together with your agent, eating ice cream—she must be asking herself what on earth is going on."

"I'm asking myself the same question," Gideon grumbled.

Dylan turned to Adrienne. "If you do end up staying a couple more days, you really shouldn't miss the festival. You'll learn a lot about the town. If Gideon won't take you, since parties aren't his thing, I would be happy to escort you."

Gideon could hardly believe his ears. Was this joker actually asking Adrienne out—right here in front of him? "I'll take her if she wants to go," he snapped.

Adrienne looked at him with raised eyebrows. Because he'd had about all of this conversation he could stand, he nodded toward the empty ice cream dishes. "Are you two finished? We'd better be going."

Dylan glanced at his watch. "I've got to go, too. I go on duty in a couple of hours."

"Really? I thought you worked the day shift," Adrienne said.

"Honesty has a very small police force," Dylan replied with a crooked smile. "We trade shifts fairly regularly."

"In other words, he works whenever his uncle the police chief tells him to," Gideon murmured.

For the first time a glint of irritation appeared in Dylan's eyes, but he managed to hold on to the smile for Adrienne. "There is that," he agreed congenially. "Those of us who have to work for a living have to answer to the boss. Not everyone can be a trust-fund baby."

Gideon had to swallow a growl, which he did only for

Isabelle's sake, as the child was looking questioningly from him to Dylan and back.

Adrienne sighed lightly and shook her head. "It was nice while it lasted," she said, obviously referring to the very brief truce between Gideon and Dylan.

He noticed that she watched as Dylan ambled away, and he couldn't help wondering if she was admiring the other guy's butt or some stupid thing like that. And then he cursed himself viciously for acting like a jealous fool, when he had absolutely no right to be jealous over Adrienne.

"What's the matter, Gideon?" Isabelle asked somewhat anxiously. "You look mad."

He made a massive effort to smooth his expression. "No, I'm not mad. I was just…thinking about something."

He avoided Adrienne's eyes for a moment, just in case his perceptive agent caught a lingering trace of wholly masculine—and totally inappropriate—possessiveness in his expression.

Chapter Eight

"The feud between you and Dylan is absolutely ridiculous," Adrienne told Gideon later. Exhausted from her tantrum and her movie outing, Isabelle had gone to bed right after dinner, leaving Adrienne and Gideon alone in the kitchen drinking coffee. "I've never seen so much measuring and muscle flexing in such a short time."

He gave her a look, then shrugged. "I've wasted enough time on Smith today. Did you have a chance to read any of my manuscript last night?"

"Almost all of it," she replied, resigned to the fact that he wasn't going to discuss Dylan. "I couldn't sleep last night, so I read for quite a while."

"And?"

She'd known all day that this question was coming. She'd spent all day trying to decide how to answer it. "It's a great story. I couldn't stop turning the pages."

He didn't look particularly pleased by her praise. "Something's bugging you about it. What?"

She eyed him warily, knowing exactly how he felt about anyone critiquing his writing. Yet he *had* asked. "It's Alanya."

"Alanya?" Gideon frowned in surprise at the mention of one of his characters. "What about her?"

"Why did you kill her?"

A frown creased his forehead. "I didn't kill her. Prater did."

"You know what I mean. What was the purpose of killing her?"

"I don't know." Looking both annoyed and puzzled, he searched for words. "It just seemed like a good dramatic turn for the story to take at that point. Gave Jackson more reason to hate Prater. More of a drive for revenge."

She nodded slowly. "I understand that, of course, but…well…"

"Well, *what?*"

"The book seemed to lose something after Alanya died. Spark, tension, diversity. I don't know. Something."

"Oh, that's very helpful."

She didn't take offense at his snarl. She, as well as anyone, understood a writer's protectiveness toward his creative vision. "Keeping her alive wouldn't involve much rewriting, would it? I mean, you really haven't gotten so far since she died."

The look he gave her then would have singed her eyelashes had she not been prepared for it. She had a strong suspicion that Gideon's struggle with this book had begun immediately after the gripping, intense, emotional—but in her opinion, unfortunate—death scene. In fact, she *knew* that was the exact point where he had run into trouble. She could see it in his writing.

He shoved himself abruptly to his feet, his chair clattering noisily against the tile floor. "Oh, no, that's no big deal at all. Simply bring a character back to life, work her into a storyline that wasn't plotted with her in it, change every damned scene to include her. Piece of cake. And why? Because my agent likes her."

He was pacing now, his hands flying as he vented his frustration. "I suppose you want a big, sloppy, romantic scene at the end. Just like Carla at the diner suggested? Something Hollywood would turn out?"

"Well…"

"Damn it." He swept a hand over the counter, knocking over a roll of paper towels and a salt-and-pepper set. A few more colorful curses followed as he stomped from one end of the kitchen to the other.

Sipping her coffee, Adrienne watched him warily. She had confidence that he would eventually see that she was right. Well, maybe confidence was too strong a word. But she *was* right. She knew she was. Not only was she an experienced agent with a good grasp of the market, she was also a reader who loved his books. This one had the potential to be the best of them all—if he kept Alanya alive. She was the strongest, most vibrant, most complex and interesting female character he had ever written, and Adrienne wanted her back.

Pushing a hand through his hair, he spun to glare at her. "You really think letting her die was a mistake? Even after I explained my reasons for doing so?"

"I really do. I think the readers are going to have a hard time accepting her death—she's such a fascinating character. She and Jackson are a powerful team, drawn together even as their differences and their equally forceful personalities work to keep them apart. The love scene you wrote just before her death—wow. It was one of the most intensely erotic scenes I've ever read, and you managed it in only a few not-particularly-explicit paragraphs. I simply don't want to accept that they won't be able to defeat their enemies together. No matter how brilliantly you conclude the story, Jackson's victory will always feel hollow to me.''

''I don't write romances, Adrienne. I've never believed that a book has to end happily to be good.''

''Neither do I. But the ending must satisfy the reader. And, trust me on this, your readers are going to want Alanya to survive. I know this because I *am* one of those readers, and I feel rather passionately about it.''

She had risen to face him during her persuasive speech, one hand resting lightly on the back of her chair to support her injured ankle. Gideon stood for what seemed like a long time just staring at her with no particular expression on his face, making her wonder if he was considering her suggestion or choosing the words he would use to fire her.

The words he finally spoke took her by surprise. ''The sex scene turned you on, huh?''

She felt her cheeks warm, an unusual occurrence for her, since she didn't usually blush easily. Must be because his question had caught her off guard. ''I called it a love scene, and I said it was beautifully written. I didn't…''

He had moved soundlessly toward her as she spoke, and her voice had grown weaker with each step he had taken, until it finally faded completely. She gazed up at him when he stopped directly in front of her. ''Gideon…''

''Have I mentioned lately that I think you're very good at your job?''

From his deep, silky tone, he could have been waxing lyrical about her eyes or her lips. The fact that he had chosen to compliment her competence was much more seductive. She had spent so much of her life trying to prove herself, with so few meaningful validations along the way. This one meant a great deal to her.

Trying to mask her emotions behind a brusquely professional facade, she asked, "Does this mean you agree with my suggestion?"

"It means I'm going to think about it. And that I appreciate everything you've done for me this week, even if I haven't made that clear before."

Her fingers tightened around the back of the chair. "I think you've done as much for me. Frankly, I needed a break from work. It took a sprained ankle and a toddler's tears to keep me here, but I've actually enjoyed the visit."

He surprised her again. "Then stay a while longer. You have another week of vacation. You know if you go back to New York, you'll only end up working."

She cautioned herself not to misinterpret his invitation. "You need help with Isabelle so you can finish your book. I understand. I suppose I could—"

"This has nothing to do with Isabelle," he refuted a bit roughly. "I can deal with her."

"Then why?"

"Because I don't want you to go yet."

The admission seemed difficult for him to make. She swallowed, wondering what, exactly, he meant by it and how, exactly, she should respond.

He seemed to feel the need for further explanation. "The, uh, the St. Patrick's Day festival Saturday," he blurted. "You said it sounds like fun. I'll take you. You can't spend a vacation in Mississippi without getting a sample of local flavor."

"But I thought you disliked that sort of thing. Dylan said—"

The unfortunately timed reference made him scowl. "I don't give a damn what Smith said. He doesn't know me half as well as he thinks he does. So what do you say? Will you stay through the weekend?''

It wasn't very hard for her to come up with an answer, after all. She wasn't ready to leave just yet. ''Yes, I'll stay. I would love to attend the St. Patrick's Day festival with you.''

His mouth tilted into a rueful smile. ''It's hardly on a scale with the St. Paddy's Day festivities in New York or Boston, but it will probably be…interesting.''

''I'm sure it will be,'' she agreed, but she wasn't sure she was talking about the festival.

His gaze holding hers, he reached up to run his fingertips lightly down the side of her cheek, reminding her of the way he had traced her face before. It was a gesture she had mentally replayed many times since, a memory that never failed to make her shiver. Just as she shivered now.

She could see that he was thinking about kissing her. And she was thinking about letting him, professional relationship be damned. His mouth was only an inch away from hers, and she felt herself swaying forward, her lips already tingling in anticipation.…

''Miss Corley?'' Isabelle's sleepy voice came from the kitchen doorway, breaking Adrienne and Gideon apart as effectively as a bucketful of cold water. ''I had a bad dream.''

Adrienne turned too quickly, sending a spiral of pain from her ankle all the way up to her hip. Clenching her jaw to hold back an expletive, she waited a beat before speaking to the child. ''I'm sorry you had a bad dream, Isabelle. Would you like a glass of water before I take you back to bed?''

Gideon was already moving toward the sink. Adrienne wasn't quite ready to look at him yet, so she concentrated on Isabelle. The little girl wasn't crying, but her expression was somber again, completely opposite to the contented smile she had worn when she'd fallen asleep.

It didn't take a child psychologist to conclude that the bad dream was in some way connected to the incident that had upset her at school. Apparently, the movie outing hadn't worked miracles, after all.

Isabelle drank a few sips of water from the glass Gideon handed her, then handed it back to him. She took Adrienne's hand, clinging tightly enough to cut off the circulation to her fingers. "I guess I'm ready to go back now," Isabelle whispered.

"Do you want me to come, too, Isabelle?" Gideon asked as they moved toward the kitchen door.

"No, thank you," she replied without looking around. "Miss Corley can tuck me in."

Glancing over her shoulder, Adrienne thought she saw Gideon recoil a bit from the casual rebuff, but she decided he must have been reacting in relief, instead. After all, this was exactly the sort of thing he wanted her there to help him handle, she reminded herself. He didn't like getting overly involved with messy emotional scenes—in his writing *or* his real life.

Isabelle climbed into the bed willingly enough, but then immediately reached for Adrienne's hand again. "Don't leave yet."

To rest her ankle, Adrienne lowered herself to the side of the bed. "I'll stay for a little while."

She smoothed tangled, baby-fine, blond tresses away from the child's warm little face. "Do you want to talk about your bad dream?"

Isabelle didn't immediately answer. And then she shook her head. "I don't think so."

"Okay. Then how about if I read you a story?"

"Could you read me one of Gideon's stories?"

Adrienne laughed softly. "Well, no. Gideon's books are rather long for bedtime, and they aren't written for children."

Isabelle looked disappointed. "Oh."

"I suppose I could *tell* you one of Gideon's stories," Adrienne said on a sudden inspiration.

"You could?"

"Yes. I know his books very well. I'm sure I can condense one of them into a bedtime story."

Isabelle pulled the covers to her chin and settled more comfortably into the pillows. "Okay."

In a quiet, soothing voice, Adrienne launched into a tale of two ancient, magical races who lived among humans, hiding their true identities while waging war with each other. She left out the gorier parts, of course. And in her version of the story, brave, noble Alanya remained alive, and she and her heroic lover, Jackson, lived happily ever after. By the time she reached that cheery resolution, Isabelle was sound asleep.

Tucking the covers more snugly around the little body, Adrienne leaned over to brush a soft kiss against Isabelle's cheek. She stood very carefully to keep from jostling the bed, then turned toward the doorway. She hadn't expected to find Gideon standing there, his long, lean body propped against the door frame, his arms crossed over his chest.

After a momentary hesitation, she stepped quietly out into the hallway. He followed her several feet away from the bedroom before he spoke. "I told you, I don't write romances."

She smiled a bit self-consciously. "I had to adjust it somewhat to make it a suitable bedtime story for a little girl."

"So you just happened to tell it the way you want it to end."

She shrugged. "I thought she would like it best that way, too."

"Did she tell you what the bad dream was about?"

"No. She didn't want to talk about it."

Frowning, he squeezed the back of his neck with one hand. "Why do I have the feeling she's not going to want to go to school again tomorrow?"

"I'm afraid you're right. This bad dream must have something to do with whatever happened at school."

"Man, I wish Mom or Nathan would get back. This thing with Isabelle is starting to worry me."

"Me, too," she admitted.

"If it's still going on tomorrow, I'm calling Mom. I hate to add to her worries, but I'm out of my league here."

"So am I."

He nodded. "We'll call her tomorrow, then."

"If we don't solve the problem on our own first," she amended, clinging to a shred of optimism.

They paused beside the door to his bedroom. In a nervous gesture, Adrienne laced her fingers in front of her. "I might as well turn in. I didn't sleep much last night, and we both need to be well rested when we face the morning."

He studied her for a moment. "Back in the kitchen, before Isabelle interrupted us?"

She swallowed, remembering the moment all too well. Maybe he was going to caution her about not complicating their business association just to satisfy their curiosity. Or lust. Or whatever the heck was building between them. If so, the warning wasn't necessary.

"Don't worry," she said, keeping her smile bright and her chin high. "I won't give it another—"

His mouth was on hers before she could complete the lie.

It didn't surprise her a bit that Gideon's kiss was powerful enough to curl her hair. This was exactly the way she had imagined he would kiss—and she had been fantasizing about it ever since she had arrived here and gotten her first good look at him. Nor was her response entirely unexpected; she wanted nothing more than to grab his shirt collar and drag him into the bedroom behind her. *His* bedroom, in which she had been sleeping alone for too many nights.

The same inclination was mirrored in his heated green eyes when he finally lifted his head. "I really wish I hadn't done that."

That was not what she had expected him to say. "Um, why not?"

He set her firmly away from him. "Because I'm about to face another sleepless night, and, as you pointed out, we need our rest. If you hear anyone pacing the hallways before dawn, it's only me. But keep your door locked, anyway."

He was trying to lighten the moment—or perhaps lessen the importance of the kiss—with a touch of dry humor. Attempting to respond in kind, she asked, "And if I leave the door open?"

"That could be taken as an invitation," he replied evenly.

She studied him for a beat before nodding and stepping back into the bedroom. "I'll keep that in mind," she said, and closed the door firmly in his face.

The bedroom door remained closed all night. Gideon knew because he checked. Several times. He just happened to be walking by, of course.

It was probably for the best, since his life was complicated enough at the moment. But, judging from that all-too-brief kiss, it would have been worth some complications.

To take his mind off what he could be doing with Adrienne, he turned his thoughts to Isabelle as he lay on the big couch in his office, staring up at the shadowy ceiling. He figured there was a good chance she would rebel against going to school again in the morning. For one thing, they had made it too pleasant for her to stay home today. And for another, they still hadn't solved whatever problem she'd had in the first place.

Adrienne's plan hadn't worked out. Isabelle had certainly enjoyed the movie, but it hadn't relaxed her enough to open up about her issues at school. And that nightmare must mean that something was still eating at her. He was beginning to think a firmer hand was called for. The kid was only four, for crying out loud, and they had been tiptoeing around her as if she were the queen of England or something.

He tried to remember what his own parents had done on occasions in his youth when he had decided he didn't want to go to school. As he recalled, his mother had taken his temperature and if it had been normal, she'd simply informed him that he was going to school and she didn't want to hear any arguments about it.

No amount of griping or whining would get him out of it, but it *would* curtail his favorite after-school activities. Every ten minutes of protesting had earned him half an hour alone in his room without his stereo, his television or his old Atari game system. Once she had figured out he was perfectly content to stay in his room with his books or his notebooks, she had changed the punishment to time spent pulling weeds from her flower beds—a chore he had detested.

He hadn't missed much school.

Lenore had been firm but fair, meting out rewards as generously as punishment. Stuart McCloud, on the other hand, had set standards that Gideon had found impossible to meet. It hadn't been as tough for Nathan, who had been content to follow his father's advice to enter law school. And Deborah could do no wrong in Stuart's eyes, with the exception, of course, of getting involved with Dylan Smith, the only thing she had ever done in outright defiance of their father's wishes.

When that romance had ended badly, and painfully, Deborah had listened to Stuart's I-told-you-sos and modeled herself into the dutiful daughter again—until Stuart had shattered her faith in him, and perhaps in all men, by betraying her trust in him.

But even before the affair and divorce that had shattered the family, Stuart and Gideon had never gotten along. Nothing Gideon ever did was good enough, none of his dreams practical enough to suit Stuart, a man who had lived to lead and impress others, his eyes firmly focused on the governor's mansion. He had expected his offspring to be ambitious, conformist and popular. For Nathan and Deborah, those things had come easily. But for Gideon— the moody, introspective, unsociable rebel—they were unbearable.

Gideon's choice to attend a public state university to study a liberal arts curriculum had been bad enough, in Stuart's eyes. Dropping out in his junior year to live on a modest trust fund from his maternal grandparents and pursue a career writing pulp fiction had pretty much severed any remaining ties between them. Rather than encouraging his younger son's dream, Stuart had belittled it, predicting failure, poverty and misery.

As far as Gideon knew, Stuart had never read anything he'd published. And Gideon had always told himself he didn't care.

Impatiently shoving those unwanted memories to the back of his mind, he rolled on the couch to check the time. Almost 5:00 a.m. Might as well get up and make a pot of coffee, maybe get a few pages written before it was time to wake Isabelle. Hell of a lot more productive use of his time than brooding over his father's parental shortcomings.

And what did the past have to do with anything, anyway? Gideon wasn't trying to be a father to Isabelle—he'd failed to learn that particular skill along the way. He'd never even pictured himself with kids, considering he would be as lousy at the task as his own dear old dad had been. All he wanted to do now was be a reasonably competent big brother and baby-sitter until someone more qualified returned to take the responsibility off his hands.

Chapter Nine

Adrienne completely understood what Gideon was trying to do Friday morning. They had tried her idea of catering to Isabelle, in hopes that she would get over her problems at school, and it hadn't worked. Now Gideon was trying the firm, serious, adult-in-charge approach.

That wasn't working, either.

"I don't want to go to school!" Isabelle shouted through a storm of tears. "I don't want to."

"You might as well accept that you have to go to school," Gideon answered flatly, his hands on his hips and a look of severely strained patience on his face. "Your nanna and Nathan are trusting me to take you to school, and I'm not going to let them down. And neither are you. Now, if there's a problem at school, you can tell me about it and I'll see what I can do to resolve it. If you refuse to tell me, you'll just have to go and try to handle it yourself."

"You can't fix it," Isabelle muttered, hanging her head. She looked so miserable that Adrienne was tempted to pick her up and cuddle her and tell her she didn't have to do anything she didn't want to do, but all that would accomplish would be to undermine Gideon's efforts.

"How do you know I can't fix it?" Gideon asked. "You haven't given me a chance. I know I'm not Nathan, but I'm not entirely incompetent."

Isabelle only sniffled.

Adrienne couldn't stay silent any longer. "Sweetheart, won't you *please* tell us what happened to upset you at school? Gideon and I want to help you, but we can't if we don't know what's wrong."

Swiping the back of one hand across her nose, Isabelle seemed to consider her next words.

Gideon produced a tissue. His tone was as firm as before, but perhaps a few degrees warmer. "Use this, and then spill it."

Though she obediently blew her nose, Isabelle looked a bit confused.

"Tell us what happened," Adrienne translated.

It seemed like a very long time before the child spoke. When she did, her question floored both Adrienne and Gideon. "Was my daddy a bad man?"

Gideon recovered first. "What are you talking about?"

His sharp tone made Isabelle draw back, looking up at him nervously.

Adrienne gave him a warning glance before speaking to the child. "Did someone say something about your father?"

Inching a bit closer to Adrienne, Isabelle nodded.

"Who was it?" Gideon demanded. "One of the kids?"

Isabelle spoke so softly that they had to strain to hear her. "A boy named Danny. He's having a birthday party this weekend, but he said his mommy wouldn't let me come because my daddy was a bad man who hurt people. Danny said my daddy had to run away because nobody wanted him here anymore and they don't want me, either. And another boy named Bryson said his grandma feels sorry for Nanna because Nanna didn't want me here, either.''

Gideon's jaw was so tight Adrienne could almost hear his teeth grind together. "Did you tell any of your teachers what the little bas—er, jerks said?''

"No. 'Cause then they would have called me a tattletale, and everyone makes fun of tattletales.''

"Hell, it's no wonder you don't want to go back there. It's a school full of morons.''

Her wet eyes going round, Isabelle looked uncertainly up at Adrienne. "Gideon said the *h* word,'' she whispered.

"Yes, dear. He's upset because your feelings were hurt. Your brother doesn't like it when people hurt his little sister.''

Gideon's eyes snapped green fire. "What's Danny's last name?''

Isabelle shrugged. "I don't know.''

"You can bet I'll find out.'' He reached for the truck keys hanging on a hook by his back door. "You stay home. I'll go to the school.''

Adrienne reacted hastily. "Isabelle, go watch TV or something. I need to talk to Gideon.''

"You'll keep an eye on her until I get back, won't you?'' Gideon was moving toward the door even as Isabelle left the room. "I don't expect to be gone very long.''

"Gideon, wait. We need to discuss what you're going to say. You need to calm down before you go charging to the school.''

He didn't pause. "I know exactly what I'm going to say."

Adrienne stepped between him and the door, placing herself so that he would have to move her aside to leave. "Stop."

He studied her through narrowed eyes. "What?"

This was not the man who had kissed her so warmly and thoroughly last night. The man she faced now was coldly, dangerously furious. Focusing only on the present moment, she shook her head. "You can't go to the school when you're this angry. You don't even know the last names of the children who said those things."

"I'm damned well going to find out." He took another step forward, but she stood her ground, leaving them almost toe-to-toe.

"I agree that the administration should be made aware of what happened. But you don't want to cause so much trouble that you make things worse for Isabelle when she goes back."

"*If* she goes back. Why the hell should she stay in a school that allows her to be subjected to that?"

"But that's not really your decision to make, is it? Isn't Nathan Isabelle's legal guardian?"

That made him frown. "I'm as much her brother as Nathan is. In his absence, it's up to me to make sure she's well treated."

As much as she admired his determination to defend and protect Isabelle—coming from Gideon, that seemed quite a concession—she wasn't sure he was thinking clearly enough to be logical and rational.

"Nathan is her legal guardian," she repeated. "You really shouldn't make any drastic moves without discussing them with him first."

Her reasoning finally seemed to get through the haze of

anger that had gripped him. Scowling, he squeezed the back of his neck with one hand. "Damn it."

She took that as a reluctant admission that she was right. "Maybe you should call your brother before you speak to someone at the school."

"I guess you're right. I shouldn't be dealing with this, anyway. As you said, Nathan's the one who brought Isabelle here and made himself responsible for her. I never agreed to get involved."

"But you are involved, aren't you?" She gave him a sympathetic smile. "You love her."

His scowl deepened. Visibly uncomfortable with the emotionalism she had just expressed, he backed off a step. "She's a good kid. She doesn't deserve to be hurt that way."

"No, she doesn't. You should go in and talk to her."

What might have been a touch of panic flashed across his face. "*I* should talk to her?"

"Of course. This concerns your family history. She needs to hear the story from someone who cares about her, rather than the gossip she'll overhear around town."

"Maybe it would be better if Nathan has that talk with her. After all, he stayed on speaking terms with Dad."

"Oh, *now* you want to wait for Nathan."

He looked downright sheepish then—an expression that didn't sit particularly well on him. "He's better at that sort of thing. Heart-to-heart talks, I mean."

"Whereas, you feel perfectly qualified to go to Isabelle's school and raise hell."

"Well...yeah."

"I see."

He looked toward the kitchen doorway, a muscle working in his jaw. "How am I supposed to tell her the details of her parents' clandestine courtship?"

"What has she already been told?"

"I'm not sure, exactly. I assume she knows my parents divorced and that she was the product of our father's second marriage."

"You can explain to her that there are always painful emotions when a marriage ends. That your mother, her nanna's, feelings were hurt, but she got over it and she's grown to love Isabelle very much."

He thought about it a minute, then nodded. "I can tell her that stuff, but I would have thought she already knew it."

"Maybe she simply needs reassurance that her father wasn't a bad man, and that your mother was looking forward to having Isabelle with her this week. And you should remind her again that your parents' divorce and your father's remarriage is no one else's business." She couldn't keep the indignation out of her voice when she added the latter.

"You can bet I'll tell her that."

"The only thing I don't understand is why other people are so vicious about the divorce. I'm sure there was some gossip at the time, but it's not as if divorce is all that uncommon, even around here, surely."

"It is when a gubernatorial candidate leaves his wife and family for a pregnant campaign volunteer half his age."

"Good lord." She stared at him. "Your father was a candidate for governor?"

He nodded grimly. "Probably would have won, if he'd have kept his pants zipped for a few more months. He was ahead in the polls, a real favorite of the media."

"You father was almost governor of Mississippi." She was stunned that she hadn't heard about this before, but then, she hadn't really talked to many locals during her time here. She had been focused almost entirely on Gideon and Isabelle.

He massaged the back of his neck. "Needless to say, the people who had donated countless hours of their time and generous chunks of their paychecks to support his campaign were not happy with him for throwing it all away so late in the game. His party had to scramble to find a replacement candidate—who lost, by the way—and the media had a field day with the gossip. My mother was humiliated, my sister was devastated and many of the locals acted as betrayed as his family felt. It was fairly ugly."

He had never sounded more lazily Southern, which meant, she decided, that he was hiding a great deal of emotion behind that detached drawl. "I'm sorry, Gideon. That must have been a horrible time for all of you."

Looking away, he shrugged one shoulder. "We got through it. It wasn't as hard for me as it was the others, I think, because I was already estranged from my father. And already accustomed to being the subject of local gossip."

She didn't entirely believe him. His father's defection had probably been just as hard for Gideon. He had spent all those years struggling in vain to fit an image of perfection outlined by a man who had been revealed to have major weaknesses of his own. And then Stuart had died before Gideon could resolve any of the issues between them.

How many times had he mentally said goodbye to his father prior to that last, final farewell? And had he grieved each time or had the estrangement been a series of blows that had left permanent scars on his heart?

Because she knew he would resist any offers of sympathy concerning his father, she concentrated on Isabelle instead. "There are people in this town who still harbor so much resentment against Isabelle's parents that they would reject an innocent child?"

"Frankly, I was concerned about that when Nathan brought her here. I knew she would hear the gossip eventually, though I never thought it would come this soon. Most of the townspeople took their cues from my mother. At first she was violently opposed to Nathan taking Isabelle in. I think she saw it as a betrayal of his loyalty to her—a painful reminder that he hadn't cut Dad off after the divorce, the way the rest of us had. She worried that Nathan was making too great a sacrifice by taking responsibility for Isabelle. At the time, Nathan and Caitlin hadn't become an item yet, and Mom thought Nathan would be raising Isabelle on his own, which he seemed perfectly willing to do."

"I don't suppose he felt as though he had any other choice."

"Actually, he gave some thought to putting her up for adoption when her guardian in California was no longer able to care for her. At the time there seemed to be few other options, and Nathan wasn't sure he was qualified to take her. But when it came right down to decision time, he couldn't give her up."

Just the thought of little Isabelle being turned over to strangers made Adrienne's stomach clench. "Of course he couldn't. You would have made the same decision."

Gideon looked a bit surprised. "I don't know about that."

Glancing toward the empty doorway, Adrienne lowered her voice. "Be honest, Gideon. If you had to make a choice right now of taking full responsibility for your sister or giving her up to strangers, never to see her again, you would make the same choice your brother made."

Obviously, his first instinct was to disagree. She watched as the realization slowly hit him that she was probably right. Now that he had spent time with Isabelle, had grown to know her and care about her, he wouldn't find it easy to walk away from her.

He wouldn't like admitting—even to himself—that he'd let his little sister become that important to him. Gideon seemed to view love as a bond and he allowed very few people to have that sort of tie to him. Maybe that was why he'd backed off so quickly after kissing *her*—not that the kiss had had anything to do with love, she added quickly. He simply didn't welcome any emotional entanglements, even...well, whatever had spurred that kiss.

"Go talk to her," she urged, concentrating once more on the problem at hand. "Tell her she *is* wanted here. You don't have to go into details if you think that should be left to Nathan, but at least make her feel like she belongs."

Looking as though he would rather endure a root canal, he shoved a hand through his hair. "Go with me."

"Wouldn't you rather talk to her in private? This is family business, after all."

"It's not as if there are any secrets left," he said impatiently. "Come talk to her with me. She's attached to you, and I don't always make myself clear."

If her presence would make this difficult conversation easier for him, she supposed it wouldn't hurt for her to sit quietly in the background.

Isabelle was curled on the couch when they entered the den, but she wasn't watching television. She held a book instead. *Green Eggs and Ham,* by Dr. Seuss, Adrienne noted. She had already learned that it was Isabelle's favorite book. Adrienne fully identified with turning to a favorite book for comfort during times of stress. She had been doing so for most of her life.

She took the chair farthest from the couch, settling silently into it while Gideon perched awkwardly next to Isabelle. "About what those jerk kids said to you—"

"You mean Danny and Bryson?" she asked.

"Yeah. Danny and Bryson." He practically spat the names.

"What about them?"

"They're full of beans."

His blunt assessment made Isabelle smile a little. "That sounds funny."

"It means they were wrong. Nathan and Caitlin and Nanna and I aren't sorry you're here in Honesty with us. You're a McCloud, and we take care of our own."

Adrienne swallowed a sigh. What made this man who possessed such an amazing mastery of words on paper come across so stilted and awkward in face-to-face conversations? He sounded as though he were quoting a family-loyalty speech from one of those old TV Westerns.

Isabelle gazed up at her brother with a puzzled look puckering her little face. "Was my daddy really a bad man?"

Adrienne held her breath while Gideon mentally debated his answer.

"No," he said. "Your father wasn't a bad man. He made some mistakes, and he made a few people mad, but he wasn't bad. And I know he was crazy about you."

Adrienne smiled at him to show her approval of his choice of words. He gave her a brusque nod, then turned his attention back to Isabelle.

"How did he make people mad?"

There was another pause before he answered again. "You'll hear more details about that later. Let's just say there were some hard feelings when he and my mother broke up. But Mom doesn't blame you for anything, Isabelle.''

"Nanna doesn't wish I wasn't here?"

"Nanna is very happy you're here," he replied firmly. "She thinks of you as her first grandchild."

Isabelle thought about that for a moment, then looked at Adrienne, as if seeking a second opinion.

"If Gideon says it, you know you can believe it," Adrienne assured her. "Gideon doesn't tell polite fibs."

Even a four-year-old had to concede that. Isabelle nodded solemnly. "Gideon isn't very polite."

Adrienne tried not to laugh, but she couldn't help it. Gideon looked so befuddled, as if he weren't quite sure whether he'd just been complimented or insulted.

Isabelle looked up at him through her long eyelashes. "I like you, anyway," she said, just in case she had hurt his feelings.

His expression became even odder then, and Adrienne thought he might have been touched by Isabelle's innocent sincerity. "Er, thanks," he said, typically brusque. "Now, what about school today? Are you going to let a couple of jerks keep you away, or are you going to let them see that the McClouds don't care what anyone says about them?"

Isabelle hugged her book more tightly. "You think I should go?"

"Yeah, I think you should go. If you don't, Danny and that other creep are going to think you believe all that bull—er, garbage they said to you. And you don't, right? You believed what I told you instead."

Isabelle nodded. "But I'd be late if I went today, wouldn't I?"

He glanced at his watch. "Only a few minutes late. I'll

go in with you and tell Miss Thelma that it's my fault we're late. She'll believe that, trust me.''

"C'mon, Isabelle, I'll help you get ready," Adrienne offered, rising to her feet. "You have friends at school that you like, don't you? Kelsey and Jessica and Justin?"

She remembered those names from earlier conversations. Gideon, who probably hadn't remembered any of them, looked a bit impressed when Isabelle nodded. "Those are my best friends. And Tiffany."

"Good. Then you play with your friends who like you because of who you are and ignore the ones who choose to be mean just to make other people feel bad. There will always be people who are nice and people who aren't. The trick is to be one of the nice ones and stay away from the mean ones as much as possible."

Isabelle dimpled up at Adrienne as she took her hand. "You're one of the nice ones," she said sweetly.

Swallowing a lump in her throat, Adrienne smiled. "So are you, sweetie."

She glanced at Gideon, who was watching them with an expression she couldn't read. "We'll be right back," she told him.

He nodded. "I'll be waiting for you."

Something in his voice made her look at him again, but there was no clue to his feelings on his face. Feeling him watching her, she led Isabelle out of the room.

Gideon seemed to have had his fill of other people that morning. He headed for his office the minute he returned from taking Isabelle to school, and Adrienne sensed he didn't plan to come out again until it was time to return for her.

She moved quickly to detain him before he could close

the door between them. "How did it go? Did Isabelle seem okay about staying?"

Though he looked impatient, he paused long enough to answer. "She was fine. One of her friends came running up to welcome her back and that seemed to please her."

He took another step toward his office, and she moved in front of him to ask one more question. "Did you speak to Miss Thelma about what happened?"

"Briefly."

"How did that go?"

"She said she would keep an out eye for any kids who seem to be giving Isabelle a hard time. Miss Thelma said she had been concerned when Nathan first admitted Isabelle that there would be problems because of the old scandals, but she thought that had been resolved when my mother publicly acknowledged Isabelle. Thelma seems genuinely fond of Isabelle, and I think she'll watch out for her."

"I hope you're right."

"It was a civil meeting. I managed not to lose my temper, even though I still think she's a stuffy old biddy."

Adrienne smiled. "Then, I'm very proud of you."

He hesitated a moment longer, his gaze on her mouth. She felt her smile fading.

Moving suddenly and without warning, he reached out, snagged the back of her neck and planted a firm kiss on her lips. "Thanks for your help this morning," he said when he released her. "Now I have to get back to work."

Before she could respond, he disappeared into his office, leaving her staring rather stupidly after him. After a moment she made an effort to close her mouth and pull herself together.

Perhaps she had better concentrate on *her* work for a while, she decided. She was getting a bit too involved with this particular client; she needed to focus on her others for a few hours. She needed to be reminded that her life was in New York, not here, and that she would be returning there very soon.

Setting up her computer in his kitchen, she spread the contents of her briefcase on the table, turned on her freshly charged cell phone and settled in for a productive work session. And then she simply sat and stared at her computer screen, paying no attention to the words there.

Her mind was filled with an image of Gideon sitting on the couch beside Isabelle, gruffly assuring the child that the McClouds "take care of their own." That touching image—along with the lingering feel of his lips pressed against her—was enough to keep her distracted from work for most of the morning.

Chapter Ten

Isabelle returned from school smiling. Her friends had rallied around her, making her feel welcome among them again, and she'd had a good day, which she shared in detail with Adrienne. Gideon had returned to his office, and Adrienne had set Isabelle at the kitchen table with a glass of juice and some sliced fruit for an after-school snack.

"And *then,*" Isabelle babbled with hardly a pause for breath, "Miss Montgomery said Danny had to sit in the time-out corner because he wouldn't be good during story time. He kept punching Benjamin's arm and then he laughed when Benjamin said it hurt."

"Danny sounds like a brat," Adrienne commented, wondering what kind of parents allowed their child to behave that way.

Isabelle nodded. "I wouldn't want to go to his old birthday party, anyway. He's too mean."

"Let's just forget about Danny. Tell me more about the

good things that happened at school today. The people who were nice to you.''

Isabelle complied happily enough. "Tiffany got her hair in braids. There were a bunch of them, with little bows at the end. It was pretty. And Justin got a new watch. It has Spiderman on it, and it tells the time in numbers because Justin doesn't know how to tell time on the other kind of clock yet. I don't, either, but Nate said he's going to teach me. And we're going to get a dog when Nate and Caitlin get back from their honeymoon. Caitlin and me want a little white dog.''

Though she wasn't sure how the conversation had suddenly switched from school to dogs, she followed along encouragingly. "I like dogs, myself. I used to have a silver poodle named Susie who was my very best friend when I was growing up.''

She had spent many lonely hours with that little dog after her mother died, finding the unconditional love that her father had been incapable of offering.

"Caitlin thinks we need to get a, um, something that starts with a *b*. Like beecher?''

Adrienne thought a moment, then suggested. "A bichon, maybe?''

"That's it, I think.''

"A bichon frise. They're cute little white dogs, very similar to poodles.''

"I want to name my dog Fluffy.''

"That's a lovely name.''

"But Nate says we need a big, black dog with big teeth and we should call him Killer or Spike.''

"Um…''

Isabelle giggled. "Nate likes to make jokes. He's silly sometimes.''

Remembering that Gideon had said he and his older

brother were quite different, Adrienne remarked, "Nathan sounds very nice."

"He's the best big brother in the world," Isabelle agreed fervently. And then looked suddenly stricken. "But Gideon's nice, too," she added a bit loudly, as if he might overhear.

Amused, Adrienne agreed, "Yes, he is—in his own way."

"Do *you* like Gideon, Miss Corley?"

Her eyebrows rose in reaction to the child's tone. Isabelle wasn't indulging in a bit of toddler matchmaking, was she? "Yes, I like Gideon. He's my client— I work with him to sell his books. I think he's a very talented writer."

"Are you going to marry him, like Caitlin married Nate? They work together. Caitlin's my sister now, and you would be my sister, too, if you marry Gideon. I have another sister, too. Her name is Deborah, but I don't see her very much."

All amusement gone now, Adrienne cleared her throat. "Gideon and I are friends and business associates, Isabelle. We aren't going to be married."

A flicker of disappointment crossed the child's face. "I wish you could be my sister."

"Couldn't I just be your friend instead? Everyone could use more good friends."

Isabelle nodded in resignation. "Okay, Miss Corley. I'll be your friend."

"You can start by calling me Adrienne."

Pleased, Isabelle nodded. "Okay, Adrienne. I think I'll go play now. Gideon said I could take my toys outside and sit on the swing."

"Put on a jacket, okay? That wind is a bit chilly."

"Okay." Climbing out of the chair, Isabelle dashed

from the room, leaving Adrienne to tidy the remains of the snack and spread out her work again.

She could see Isabelle through the big window over the sink. The little girl had settled into the free-standing lawn swing in Gideon's backyard with a doll, her stuffed owl and a couple of books. As she had promised, she had donned a lightweight denim jacket with her T-shirt and jeans. Her little white sneakers pumped the air to keep the swing moving as she read with animated expression to her stuffed friends.

Adrienne found herself spending more time watching Isabelle than concentrating on her work. The child made such a pretty picture, her golden curls glittering in the afternoon sun, her cheeks pinkened by the brisk March breeze.

She would be proud to have this child for a little sister, she thought.

Or a daughter.

That thought took her aback. *Whoa, Adrienne. Who wound your biological clock?*

Hoping the faint ticking would stop if she ignored it, she focused fiercely on the computer again. A rather whiny and petulant e-mail from one of her authors was on-screen and she had to figure out a way to answer it patiently, effectively and reassuringly.

Who needed kids? She already spent most of her life holding hands and averting emotional crises.

When Gideon hadn't emerged from his office by dinnertime, Adrienne took matters into her own hands and prepared a meal without consulting him. She assumed he had gotten so involved with his work that time had slipped away from him.

She hoped he had gotten more accomplished that day than she had.

Preparing a simple meal of baked pork chops with rice and vegetables, she moved around the kitchen with only an occasional twinge of pain from her ankle. The prescribed anti-inflammatories and exercises seemed to be doing the job. The swelling had gone down significantly, and though it still ached almost constantly, she didn't allow herself to dwell on the discomfort.

When the meal was ready, she set the table, sent Isabelle to wash her hands and then approached Gideon's office. She tapped firmly on the door. "Gideon?"

"What?"

Though his tone wasn't particularly encouraging, she opened the door, anyway. "I've prepared dinner. Everything's on the table."

He didn't look around from the computer. "I'll be there in a few minutes."

She knew better, of course. If she closed this door now, he would forget all about her again. "You haven't eaten since breakfast. You really should take a break. Besides, Isabelle will be disappointed if you don't join us for dinner."

He exhaled gustily and spun his chair away from the computer. "Fine. I'll come to dinner. Give me a few minutes to wash up."

She didn't take offense at his curtness. She didn't like to be interrupted when she was trying to concentrate on something, either.

If Gideon seemed unusually quiet during dinner, Isabelle made up for it with her chattering. She was as animated that evening as she had been subdued the day before, making Adrienne marvel at the mercurial resilience of childhood. She repeated nearly everything she had said to Adrienne earlier, including Danny's stint in the time-out corner, and then spent another ten minutes describing the antics of a couple of squirrels she had watched in the backyard. That somehow led her back to the subject of the dog she had been promised.

"Adrienne had a poodle named Susie," she informed Gideon. "Did you ever have a dog, Gideon?"

He shook his head. "Nathan had a couple of dogs when we were kids, but I never considered them mine."

"Why not?"

"Too much trouble. They always have to be fed or watered or walked or cleaned up after. I always had other things I wanted to do."

Isabelle considered that a moment, then said firmly, "I don't care. I want a dog. I'll take care of it all by myself."

Adrienne and Gideon exchanged a knowing look.

Oblivious to their skepticism, Isabelle kept talking, listing all the things she would do with her dog. Teach him to fetch and roll over and catch a Frisbee and jump through a hoop—those were only a few of her plans for the future Fluffy.

When they had finished eating, Isabelle dashed off to play while Adrienne began to clear away the dishes. Gideon gathered a handful of utensils to stuff into the dishwasher.

"I can clean up in here," she assured him. "There isn't much to do."

"You cooked. The meal was delicious, by the way. Least I can do is clean up. You need to get off that ankle."

"It's not too bad right now. I can tell it's getting better."

"It won't keep getting better if you overexert yourself. Go put your feet up. I'll finish in here."

Because he effectively blocked her access to the sink

and dishwasher, she gave in. Rather than leave the room, she settled at the table to watch him. "You've put in long hours today. Did you get much written?"

"Some."

His curt reply told her it hadn't been a satisfying session for him. "Have you thought any more about the changes I suggested?"

"No. I told you, your suggestion didn't fit with my vision of the book. It's a story of one man's single-minded and all-consuming quest for revenge and justice—in that order. Alanya has to die."

"Or Jackson has to *think* she's dead."

She watched his shoulders stiffen before he glared at her over his shoulder. "You're determined that I'm going to write a passionate ending to this book, aren't you?"

"Gideon, you have to understand that it's my job to help you market your work. If I think there's something you can do to make your book more successful, I would be remiss not to tell you what I think."

"If I had wanted to create generic, marketing-driven, cookie-cutter products, I'd have gone to work on some factory assembly line."

She sighed and shook her head. "You're overdramatizing a bit, aren't you? I haven't exactly asked you to prostitute yourself. I simply made a suggestion because you're having trouble finishing the book."

"Of *course* I'm having trouble finishing the book!" He slammed the dishwasher door closed. "How can I write with so many people in my house? With toddlers having emotional meltdowns and my agent nagging me to write romantic drivel?"

Elbows resting on the table, she propped her chin on her crossed hands. "Should I remind you that you invited me to stay the weekend? And that you asked me to read your manuscript and tell you what I thought?''

Her calm, dryly amused tone seemed to douse his flash of temper. He stopped pacing, shoved a hand through his tumbled hair and gave her a look that might have held a faint touch of remorse. "I'm a little stressed."

She supposed it was as close as she was going to get to an apology. "I know. You've had a difficult week."

"It would have been even more difficult if you hadn't been here to help me with Isabelle."

And *that,* she decided, was his way of saying thank-you. She smiled at him. "You're welcome."

Stopping beside her chair, he reached down to catch her wrists and pull her to her feet. "There's something else that has been distracting me from work this week."

Gripping his forearms to steady herself, she gazed up at him. "I—"

He kissed the words back into her mouth.

He wasn't holding her tightly, but their bodies were pressed together from chest to knees. She remembered her first impression of him—that he was built like an athlete. Each time she felt him against her that impression was reinforced. He was lean but roped with muscle. All male. And her response was entirely feminine.

He broke off the kiss very slowly, holding her gaze with his as he lifted his head. "I really should stop doing that."

She was still holding his arms, and she was in no hurry to release him. There was a definite possibility she would melt into a puddle at his feet if she did so. She cleared her throat. "Yes, you really should."

He kissed her again. And she tightened her fingers around his sleekly muscled arms, because she felt herself slowly beginning to puddle...

"Are you *sure* you aren't going to marry Gideon, Adrienne?'' Isabelle asked curiously from the kitchen doorway. "Caitlin kisses Nathan all the time, and they got married."

By the time the child finished speaking, Adrienne and Gideon were several feet apart. Feeling her cheeks flame, Adrienne couldn't look at Gideon. For those few, reckless moments she had forgotten all about Isabelle and she suspected that Gideon had, too. How could they have been so careless?

"Come on, Isabelle, I'll tell you another story," she said hastily, holding out a hand that wasn't as steady as she would have liked. "How about the story of Little Red Riding Hood? Would you like to hear that one?"

It seemed an appropriate choice for her, as well. She needed to be reminded of the girl who had been distracted from her planned destination by a dangerously intriguing wolf.

Gideon didn't trust himself to pace the hallway outside Adrienne's bedroom that night. This time he left the house altogether, moving outside to the lawn swing.

It wasn't exactly quiet out; frogs and other night creatures were in full voice this evening. It was a bit chilly. The slightly damp night air leached through his long-sleeved T-shirt, and his breath hung in ghostly puffs in front of him. Better than a cold shower, he decided, looking ruefully toward the darkened window of his bedroom, where Adrienne slept.

He had been particularly antsy that evening, ever since Isabelle had caught him kissing Adrienne in the kitchen. He could still hear her innocent voice saying the *m* word. He'd been as shocked as if she had uttered an expletive.

Couldn't a guy kiss an attractive woman around here without someone mentioning marriage? And kissing wasn't all he wanted to do with Adrienne Corley—not by a long shot. But whatever happened between them before she headed back to New York, he had no intention of letting it turn into anything more than a pleasant interlude between two unattached adults who happened to be attracted to each other.

He was sure he and Adrienne could explore that attraction for a few days without taking it too seriously. And after she returned to New York, they could return easily enough to the comfortably professional relationship they had shared before, maybe even consider themselves friends as well as business associates. He had remained on reasonably friendly terms with one or two ex-lovers. Though he had to admit with a wince that most had left never wanting to see him again.

Adrienne was different from the women he had known before. Smart, sophisticated, competent, independent. She wouldn't expect more than he could give her—hell, she probably wouldn't want any more. Why should she? She didn't need any man, especially a grouchy, self-centered loner like him.

He still regretted the way he had snarled at her after dinner, simply because she had asked about his work. Not that she had seemed particularly offended. Probably because she didn't care enough about him to let him hurt her feelings.

Scowling, he gave the ground a vicious kick to set the swing in motion. The resulting creak of chains startled the night creatures into silence, so that his thoughts seemed unusually loud in his head.

When could he kiss Adrienne again? Would there be any opportunity for more than kisses before she left?

And would it really be as easy to say goodbye as he'd been reassuring himself it would be?

*   *   *

Adrienne half expected Gideon to change his mind about attending the St. Patrick's Day festival on Saturday. She wouldn't have been surprised if he'd stayed in his office all day without coming out or even mentioning the festival again, leaving her and Isabelle to entertain themselves. Yet she wore her thin emerald sweater with her black slacks—just in case green was the color of the day.

She was rather relieved when he appeared at breakfast, dressed in a white button-up shirt and jeans, his neatly-combed-for-a-change hair still damp from the shower. "So are we going to that festival downtown?" he asked gruffly.

Still in her pajamas, Isabelle looked intrigued. "What festival thing?"

"The St. Patrick's Day Festival Officer Smith told us about," Adrienne reminded her. "Everyone wears green and pretends to be Irish."

"Miss Montgomery decorated our classroom with leprechauns and shamrocks for St. Patrick's Day," Isabelle said. "But it's not today, is it? Miss Montgomery said it's Monday and we can wear green to school if we want to."

"Today isn't officially St. Patrick's Day," Adrienne informed her. "I suppose the town is having the festival today because people have to go to work and to school on Monday."

"It's just an excuse for the chamber of commerce to make some money from vendors and business exhibitors," Gideon said. "For some reason, people will pay three-fifty for a hot dog and two bucks for a watered-down soda as long as you call the event a festival."

Isabelle eyed him questioningly. "You don't want to go?"

Adrienne watched him force a smile for his sister's benefit. "Sure. Can't wait."

Taking pity on him, she smiled. "I can take Isabelle to

the festival, Gideon. That would give you a chance to work in peace today. My ankle's so much better, I'm sure I could drive your truck—''

"I said I would take you to the festival and I will." The look he gave her just dared her to argue. She didn't have the nerve.

Instead she glanced at Isabelle's empty cereal bowl. "I'll help you get dressed, sweetie. I bet we can find something green for you to wear, if you like."

"Gideon isn't wearing green."

Adrienne couldn't look at him, knowing she would laugh if she did. "It isn't required. It's only for fun."

"Okay. I've got a green shirt. I'll wear that."

Following the child out of the room, Adrienne found herself almost as excited about attending the festival as Isabelle.

She doubted that Gideon would have said the same.

It was a beautiful day in Honesty, the sky a brilliant blue, the temperature climbing to a comfortable sixty-eight degrees after the chilly night. Whether it was because of the nice weather or the popularity of the event itself, a sizable crowd mingled on the streets of old downtown Honesty.

The center square had been closed to traffic, so Gideon parked in a nearby church lot and they walked the final block. Gideon had insisted that Adrienne use the crutches, though she really hadn't wanted to bother with them. Once again she wore her black loafer on her left foot and a black sock beneath the brace on her right.

Gideon stayed close to her side as they joined the crowds on the sidewalks. As if she might tumble onto her face if he wasn't there to catch her, she thought in exasperation. He instructed Isabelle to hold his hand to make sure she didn't get separated from them. Though he was gamely going along with this outing, he didn't look like a man who was prepared to have a good time, Adrienne couldn't help noticing.

The festival was a casual event, with jeans and T-shirts being the uniform of the day. A great deal of the green being worn for the occasion came in the form of camouflage print, she observed with a smile.

Vendors' booths and open-sided tents lined the streets. She and Isabelle paused to study each one, while Gideon waited patiently behind them. Ceramics, woodwork, needlework, handmade toys, dolls and musical instruments. Sunglasses and T-shirts, hunting and fishing gear, costume jewelry, candles and potpourri. Adrienne and Isabelle were intrigued by it all. What they *didn't* see were products that had anything to do with Ireland.

"Um, this is a St. Patrick's Day festival?" she asked Gideon, studying a display of wild game seasonings and camo caps and T-shirts.

"So they claim. Surprisingly enough, it's very much like the Fourth of July festival. And the Labor Day festival."

She laughed and they moved on to the next block. She was aware that people watched them, and that—thanks to the local gossip—most of them probably knew who she was. She supposed it was natural that there would be some curiosity about Gideon's New York agent, who had been sleeping in his house for the past week.

Several people greeted Gideon, and she could tell by his tone whether they were people he liked. He introduced her to a few of them, and she was warmly greeted. It seemed like a pleasant town, despite the usual drawbacks of small-town gossip, which Isabelle had already had to face.

Though it was a little early for lunch, the tantalizing

scents from the numerous food vendors piqued their appetites. The offerings included hamburgers and corn dogs, pizza, barbecue, fried chicken, Cajun dishes, turkey legs, cotton candy, funnel cakes, kettle corn and taffy. A stand in the center of the square had been festooned with big, cut-out shamrocks, and dispensed disposable bowls of corned beef and cabbage.

Amused by that token homage to Ireland, Adrienne decided to sample foods from the local area, instead. At Gideon's recommendation, they fell in line at the popular Cajun food stand. Gideon ordered crawfish gumbo, Isabelle requested fried catfish nuggets with French fries and Adrienne selected a shrimp PoBoy sandwich with a small side order of red beans and rice. The "gator-on-a-stick" was intriguing, but she wasn't quite brave enough to try it.

Numerous picnic tables had been set up in the food area, and Gideon efficiently commandeered one that had just been vacated, ignoring the disgruntled scowls from a group of teenagers who had spotted it at roughly the same time. He carried Adrienne's food for her, set it on the table, then returned for the drinks they had ordered—iced tea for the adults and lemonade for Isabelle.

Their casual meal was accompanied by a cheerful cacophony of festival sounds: laughter and conversation, babies fussing and toddlers whining, tinny music from the rides that had been set up in the next street. Several yards behind her was a stage for local entertainment—a magician, a couple of garage bands and a procession of karaoke singers, some pretty good, others a bit painful to hear, but all eager to perform.

Isabelle was almost too busy watching the activities around them to eat. Adrienne had no trouble concentrating on her food. It was delicious.

"There's a kids' area, Gideon," Isabelle said, pointing.

"They're doing face painting and giving away balloons. And there's a game where I can win prizes by picking a rubber duckie out of a wading pool. Can we go there next?"

"Yeah, I guess we—"

"And can I ride the merry-go-round? I want a black horse, because they're the prettiest. And maybe later we can have some cotton candy?"

"Sure," he said, visibly resigning himself to spending a while longer at the festival. "Why not?"

Leaving the table for other diners, they moved toward the children's area, Isabelle leading the way. Expressing concern about her overtaxing her sprained ankle, Gideon parked Adrienne on a bench with a good view of the festivities. "I'll let Isabelle play for a while. You sit here and people watch. You seem to enjoy that."

Because it was exactly what she liked most about this sort of event, she smiled, propped her crutches against the armrest of the bench and settled down for an interesting voyeuristic session. "I'll be just fine here."

Gideon allowed himself to be towed away by his excited little sister. He looked at Adrienne over his shoulder as he disappeared into the crowd, and she had to laugh softly at his lamb-led-to-the-slaughter expression. This outing was good for him, she decided. He needed to get out among people more. He was too young to be an eccentric recluse.

Not that Gideon's personal life was any of her business, of course.

"Hey, Miz Corley. Remember me?"

The woman's stiffly teased gray hair and kindly eyes were immediately recognizable. "Of course. You're Carla, from the diner."

Pleased to be remembered, Carla grinned and motioned toward the two fifty-something women who accompanied her. "These are my sisters, Gloria and Patsy. Girls, this is Gideon McCloud's agent from New York. I told you about meeting her at the diner."

From their avid nods, Adrienne suspected that Carla's sisters had heard about her in great detail. She spent the next ten minutes answering questions about New York, her job and Gideon's next book, which she told them they would just have to wait and read for themselves. No, she answered patiently to one arch question, she wasn't married, and then added that she and Gideon were friends and business associates, nothing more.

"Well, of course you aren't," Gloria—or was it Patsy?—said with a roll of her eyes. "What sane woman would want to get involved with Gideon McCloud? Sometimes I think that boy just isn't right."

"Now, Gloria," the one who must be Patsy chided, "you know artists are just different, that's all. Sure, he's a little…odd, but that's because their brains just don't work like ours."

The sisters were still arguing about whether Gideon was an eccentric genius or a spoiled bachelor after they bade Adrienne goodbye and moved on.

Adrienne was both amused and a bit bothered by the exchange. Why *had* Gideon cut himself off so determinedly from his neighbors? Was it only because of the pain of his father's scandal or was there more to it than that? She didn't accept the eccentric-author excuse—she knew too many writers who were sociable and well adjusted, despite their individual quirks.

"Excuse me, but you're Gideon McCloud's agent, right?"

A forty-something woman with flame-red hair, trendy glasses and a vivid green caftan worn with sandals stood at one end of the bench, eyeing Adrienne with an expression she knew all too well. "Yes, I am."

"I'm so excited to meet you. I just saw Gideon standing on the merry-go-round beside his little sister's carousel horse—a lot of people looked pretty surprised to see him there, I can tell you—and I figured you must be around somewhere, since I'd heard you were in town. My name is Yolanda Krump, and I just know that fate has brought us together like this."

Only if fate had a really twisted sense of humor, Adrienne thought with a silent groan, knowing exactly what was coming next.

"You see," Yolanda continued, leaning companionably against the end of the bench. "I've written a book. I'm sure if I just had a good agent, I could get it published. I just know the book would be a bestseller."

"Well, I—"

"I've sent it to several publishers already, but they returned it with rejection letters. Probably never even read it, since I don't have an agent and I live in Mississippi."

Living in Mississippi had nothing to do with it, of course. Editors had no particular bias against a writer's hometown. But Adrienne didn't try to argue. "I would be happy to look at a sample of your writing," she said politely, pulling a business card out of the small shoulder-strap purse she'd brought with her. "Feel free to send me a query letter and your first three chapters, and I'll get to them as soon as I have a chance."

"Don't you want me to tell you about my story? It's a saga about four generations of women in a cursed family. It's told mostly in vignettes and flashbacks, and a lot of it is autobiographical, since I've led a rather fascinating life. It—"

"I really can't make any decisions without seeing a

sample of your writing. Send me the chapters and I'll read them very carefully, I promise.''

''Yes, I will. But let me tell you what happens—''

'''Afternoon, Miz Corley. Yolanda.''

Dylan's familiar drawl was a welcome interruption. Adrienne looked around with a smile. ''Officer Smith. How nice to see you.''

''Dylan,'' he reminded her, taking a seat on the bench beside her. ''Are you enjoying the festival?''

''Yes, very much, thank you.''

''Dylan, I was trying to tell Miss Corley about my book,'' Yolanda began with some indignation.

He shook his head. ''Oh, I doubt that she wants to talk about work today. She's on vacation, you know.''

''Send me your chapters,'' Adrienne repeated. ''I'll get back to you as quickly as I can, though I can't give you a guarantee about representing you, of course.''

Looking dissatisfied but resigned, Yolanda nodded and bustled away, clutching Adrienne's card like a talisman.

Chapter Eleven

"I don't want to prejudice your opinion, but I think you should be prepared. The book is awful," Dylan murmured as the aspiring writer reluctantly moved away. "It's been turned down by every reputable publisher and a half dozen agents already."

"You've read it?"

He sighed gustily. "I tried. Made it through a few chapters before I couldn't stomach any more. It's boring, clichéd, grammatically butchered and darned near incoherent, plotwise. I tried telling her those things, but she dismissed everything I said by telling me I didn't know what I was talking about."

"Then why did she ask you to read it?"

"She's badgered nearly everyone in town to read it," he said with a grimace. "Even tried to convince Gideon, though, needless to say, she didn't get anywhere with him. She knew I did a little writing during high school—I worked for a newspaper—and she thought I might have a suggestion for punching up the opening so it would be more intriguing to editors. My suggestion was to burn the first three chapters, but she didn't appreciate that.''

"I'm sure she didn't. So what sort of writing did you do? Strictly newspaper articles, or did you ever try your hand at fiction?''

He shrugged and looked away, concentrating for a moment on a group of teenagers who were getting a bit rowdy. ''I played around with some fiction. Never seriously, though.''

"Really. Do you still write?''

"As a matter of fact, yes, for a hobby. But don't tell Gideon. I'm sure he would hate the idea of me dabbling even casually in his area of expertise.''

He sounded lazily amused, but Adrienne sensed that this subject wasn't entirely frivolous to him. ''What have you written?''

Looking vaguely uncomfortable, he shrugged. ''I don't want to sound like Yolanda.''

"You sound nothing like Yolanda. What do you write?''

"I like mysteries,'' he finally admitted. ''I've started a series about a small-town Southern cop who solves crimes in an unconventional way. Hardly a groundbreaking premise, of course, but it's a little different because he suffers from a couple of phobias that occasionally interfere with his job and that he tries constantly to conceal.''

"That sounds interesting. Have you actually written a complete book?''

He was practically squirming on the bench now, like an embarrassed adolescent. ''Yeah, a couple. But it's just something I do to relax when I'm not working. I'm single, no family, don't have many hobbies. Writing is something to fill the time."

"You have no interest at all in being published?"

"Sure, I've thought about it. Maybe I'll send my work out someday—when I'm ready."

"I don't suppose you would let me look at it?"

He whipped his head around to stare at her. "Why would you want to do that?"

She smiled. "Something tells me you have talent. I could be wrong, of course."

He laughed softly. "I doubt you would mince words if you didn't like it."

"I like to think of myself as tactful but honest. Not everyone likes what I have to say," she added, thinking of Gideon's resistance to her suggestions for his current book.

Seeming to follow the direction of her thoughts, Dylan glanced around as if to make sure Gideon wasn't nearby when he said, "Don't tell him I said this, but Gideon's a darned good writer. I've read and enjoyed all his books."

"Have you really?"

He nodded. "Bought the first one because I wanted to hate it. I hoped his writing would be as unexciting and unpleasant as his personality. I was wrong. The first book was so good I bought the others simply because I wanted to read them. I drove out of town to buy them, of course, then smuggled them into my house in brown paper bags. I wouldn't want word to get back to Gideon that I read his books."

"Of course not," she agreed gravely.

"Remember, you promised not to say anything to him."

"Cross my heart. Will you let me read your book?"

He groaned. "I never should have said anything about it. I really am as bad as Yolanda."

"No, because I'm the one asking you. And I warn you, Dylan, I can be very persistent."

"Are you this persistent when you're representing your clients' work?"

"Worse. Editors know they might as well hear my pitch because I'm not going to go away unheard."

"You sound like the sort of agent a writer would want on his side."

"I am. So let me read your work."

"What if you hate it?"

"Then I'll tell you so. I'll be tactful but honest," she said with a smile.

He considered it a moment, then shrugged. "Maybe. But if Gideon finds out, all hell will break loose."

"I don't know why. You aren't writing just to annoy him, are you?"

"Of course not. I didn't even know he wanted to write until he published his first book a few years back. I was living in another state then. Darn, it griped my hide that I liked it."

She laughed. "You two are ridiculous, you know that? Just because you dated his sister a long time ago is no reason two very nice men with similar interests can't be friends now."

The smile in Dylan's eyes dimmed then. "There was a bit more to it than that."

There still was more to it, Adrienne realized suddenly, reading something in his expression that he probably would have liked to keep hidden. She would bet that Dylan still had feelings for Deborah McCloud, no matter how much time had passed since their breakup.

Or was she overromanticizing again—as Gideon had accused her of trying to do to his book?

Carrying a small stuffed bear, Gideon reappeared at that

moment with Isabelle beside him. Isabelle had a shamrock painted on her cheek, a green helium-filled balloon tied to one wrist and a cone of green-tinted cotton candy in her other hand. She dimpled. "Hi, Officer Smith. Do you want a bite?"

He glanced at the rather noxiously colored spun sugar with a slight shudder, though he managed a smile. "No, thank you, Isabelle. I'd better be moving along."

"I think that's an excellent idea," Gideon muttered.

Just to make Gideon mad—Adrienne had no doubt that was the reason—Dylan leaned over to brush a friendly kiss against her cheek. "See you later, Adrienne."

He sauntered away whistling, sounding quite pleased with his exit.

Gideon was practically quivering with outrage when he took Dylan's place on the bench beside Adrienne. "That guy's really starting to tick me off."

She knew better than to smile, though she felt compelled to say, "I like him."

"I like him, too," Isabelle offered, climbing comfortably onto Gideon's knee to eat her cotton candy. Her face was already dotted with sticky bits of green fluff.

Pushing the floating green balloon out of his face, Gideon continued to glare at Adrienne. "Did he ask you out again?"

"No, he did not."

"Then why was he hanging around?"

"We were just talking."

"I think Gideon's jealous," Isabelle commented without looking away from her sticky treat.

Both Adrienne and Gideon looked at the child in surprise.

"Caitlin says Brad Pitt is cute. Nate pretends to get mad, and Caitlin says he's jealous. Are you jealous, Gideon?"

"Eat your green stuff," he muttered.

She giggled and took another big bite.

Gideon wasn't jealous, of course, Adrienne assured herself. It was just that he disliked Dylan and wasn't pleased that she had befriended him.

And then his eyes met hers over Isabelle's head, and she was shaken by the hard glint in them. She knew a look of sheer masculine possessiveness when she saw one.

Maybe Isabelle hadn't been so far off, after all.

Adrienne was not at all surprised when Gideon retreated to his office again after they returned from the festival. It was a pattern she had learned to predict—any time he felt himself getting too close to someone, he retreated into his sanctuary and made-up worlds.

She spent the evening playing board games and watching television with Isabelle. Surprisingly enough, she had a lovely evening. She hadn't spent much time around children, but Isabelle was a delight. She could certainly understand why so many people had grown to love the little girl.

When it was time for Isabelle to turn in, she wrapped her arms tightly around Adrienne's waist. "I had fun today."

Hugging the freshly bathed, sweet-smelling child, Adrienne rested her cheek against Isabelle's soft curls. She could hear that previously unnoticed biological clock ticking again. Would she ever hold a child of her own? She was twenty-eight years old and not even involved with anyone. Motherhood seemed rather unlikely at the moment.

Holding Isabelle's hand, she tapped on Gideon's office door, then pushed it open. "Isabelle wants to say goodnight."

He looked around from the computer. "Is it bedtime already?"

Isabelle padded toward his chair. "Past bedtime. Adrienne let me stay up to watch a funny movie on the Disney channel."

"Oh. Well, good night, then. Sleep well."

Since he was still seated, Isabelle was able to reach up to wrap her arms around his neck. "Thank you for taking me to the festival and buying me cotton candy and letting me ride the merry-go-round. I had fun."

He patted her back. He didn't look as awkward about it as he had only a few days earlier. "I'm glad you had a good time."

She planted a smacking kiss on his cheek. "G'night, Gideon. I love you."

Gideon cleared his throat even as Adrienne felt a lump form in her own. "Yeah," he said. "Me, too. Now run along to bed."

As she tucked Isabelle into bed, Adrienne wondered when Gideon had last said the words *I love you* to anyone. Had he hidden his tender feelings so deeply that he would never be able to find them again?

Gideon shut down his computer at midnight—not because he was tired, but because the words simply weren't coming to him. He told himself to stay in the office for the rest of the night, but he found himself prowling the hallways, anyway—just to check that everything was secured.

The outside doors were all locked, the lights all turned off. The automatic coffeemaker was set for the usual time; he wanted coffee immediately available when he stumbled into the kitchen at dawn. Isabelle was sound asleep in her bed. He tucked the covers around her and pulled the door partially closed behind him as he left.

It was only then that he noticed his own bedroom door was standing open.

He remembered telling Adrienne that leaving the door open could be interpreted as an invitation. Surely she had just forgotten to close it. Maybe she had gotten a bit too warm in there.

He was getting pretty damned hot himself.

She stepped out of the shadows of the bedroom, pausing to lean against the doorjamb with her arms crossed under her breasts. Which, by the way, were displayed quite nicely by the deeply scooped neckline of her black nightgown.

He'd thought once that she wore a bit too much black, since that seemed to be a staple of her wardrobe. Now he realized just how flattering the color was with her creamy skin and glossy auburn hair, both of which were softly illuminated by the nightlight he kept in the hallway to facilitate his habit of pacing the house during the nighttime hours.

"You, uh, couldn't sleep?" he asked, and his voice had a ragged edge to it.

Her own voice was low, probably to keep from disturbing Isabelle. The result was very intimate. "No. You, neither?"

He felt himself drawn toward her, as if by a magnetic force. He planted his bare feet firmly on the carpet to resist. "No."

She waited a bit, then smiled a little. "Why don't you come in, and we could 'not sleep' together?"

Though the sentence was rather convoluted, the meaning was clear enough. This was most definitely the invitation her open door had implied.

Because he was a normal, red-blooded male, his first instinct was to leap forward before she changed her mind. Because he was the surly and suspicious type, he asked, "Why?"

He couldn't imagine what he had done to amuse her. Her soft, unpainted lips curved into a faint smile. "Well...if you aren't interested..."

"I didn't say that. I'm just curious about what you have in mind."

Her smiled deepened at the corners, and she took a step toward him. "What I have in mind is seducing you. And if you haven't figured that out by now, then I must be losing my touch."

The surge of heat through his body confirmed that she had not lost her touch. "I, er, got that," he managed to say coherently. "My question, again, is...why?"

She placed a hand on his chest. A muscle jumped beneath his skin. He wished now that he had kept his shirt on with his jeans. Standing there barefoot and bare-chested made him feel oddly vulnerable. As if he were, indeed, being seduced.

She watched her own hand as it slid up his chest to his shoulder. "Does it matter why?"

A faint echo of Isabelle's innocent comments about marriage and jealousy sounded in the back of his mind. "Maybe."

Resting her other hand on his other shoulder, she gazed up at him through her lashes. "I'll be going back to New York in a day or two. Do you really want this to end with the few kisses we've shared?"

No, he most definitely did not want it to end with those kisses. He had fully intended to plot his way into her bed—*his* bed—before she left. So why was he suddenly hesitating when it seemed she was offering him a no-strings opportunity to scratch a growing itch, satisfy their curiosity or whatever it would be?

Her hands were looped behind his neck now, bringing her body lightly against his. Her dark eyes gleamed like polished onyx in the shadowy hallway as her gaze held his. "Well, Gideon? Do you want me to go back inside and close the door or do you want to come inside with me? It's up to you."

Adrienne couldn't have pinpointed the moment she decided to invite Gideon into her bed—or rather, *his* bed. Maybe it had been during one of those spectacular kisses. Or perhaps at the festival, when he had been so patient and indulgent with Isabelle.

Or maybe it had been the expression in his eyes when she'd left him in his office again that night. Weariness. Discouragement with his work. Loneliness.

Emotions with which she identified all too well.

She didn't try to deceive herself that they would have more than a night or two together. But maybe a few stolen hours would give them a reason to smile during the quiet, sleepless nights ahead—for both of them.

Besides which, his kisses made her knees go weak.

Craving another of those kisses, she tilted her face invitingly upward, waiting for his decision. She understood his hesitation; Gideon was a man who guarded his emotions ferociously. She saw the brief debate take place in his eyes before he covered her mouth with his, and she realized with a heady mixture of pleasure and nerves that he had decided to accept her bold invitation.

Before her knees buckled altogether, she took a step backward, toward the open bedroom doorway. Without lifting his mouth from hers, he followed her, walking her backward through the doorway, then reached behind him to close and lock the door.

He lifted his head just far enough to ask, "You're sure about this?"

She made a face and gave a short laugh. "All I'm sure about right this moment is that I want this. I want you."

A low growl of response rumbled in his chest. He kissed her again, fiercely this time, and she sensed that her candid words had snapped the last thread of resistance he'd been clinging to. A moment later her bare feet were dangling above the floor, and then he dropped her onto the bed. She locked her arms around his neck, pulling him down with her.

His weight crushed her into the mattress, and it was a delicious feeling. Hard against soft. Curves against angles. Wrapping her legs around his, she shivered with the anticipation of how perfectly they would fit together.

Gideon was such a clever and creative man, she thought happily. This was going to be very interesting....

At the moment he was a very impatient man. His hands weren't quite steady when they swept over her—and it awed her to think that she could make this strong, controlled man tremble.

She speared her fingers into his perpetually messy dark hair, loving the thick, silky feel of it. Apparently, he hadn't seen a barber in a while—not that she minded in the least.

His lips moved against the galloping pulse in her throat, making it race even faster. His hands slid to cup her breasts, and her heart threatened to stop beating altogether. She had to remind herself to breathe.

His thumbs rotated, causing her to arch upward into his hands. Her fingers clenched convulsively in his hair. He grunted. "Ouch."

Laughing softly, breathlessly, she loosened her grip. "Sorry."

"I'm not." His mouth covered her smile, his tongue plunging between her lips to mate with his.

Amusement fading in a quick flash of heat, she moved her hands to his bare shoulders. His skin was hot, sleek. Muscles bunched and rippled beneath her palms as he moved over and against her.

She hadn't expected pretty words or sweet nothings from Gideon, and she didn't get them. He was a silent lover, but a thorough one. There wasn't an inch of her body that did not receive his attentions. Her black nightgown proved no obstacle to him; he had it off her almost before she realized it. His jeans quickly joined the swath of black fabric on the floor.

She discovered immediately afterward that Gideon was a *very* well-built man.

He kept protection in his nightstand—a fact she had discovered several days earlier. She hadn't been snooping, just looking for a safe place to keep her jewelry and contact lenses when she wasn't wearing them. Her first glimpse of those shiny silver packets had filled her mind with images that had left her hot and bothered for hours.

Her imagination hadn't come close to reality.

Mindful of the child sleeping across the hall, she bit back a cry of pleasure when he finally joined them together. She couldn't totally suppress the moan of delight that escaped when he began to move. He covered her mouth with his to smother any more sounds.

Yet at the moment of climax, it was Gideon who lost control, expressing his satisfaction with a deep, hoarse groan. Even as she gave in to her own shivering release, Adrienne was pleased by the sign that Gideon was as affected by their lovemaking as she was.

They recovered in a silence broken only by the sounds of their ragged breathing. Gideon lay on his back. While his arm was beneath her, he wasn't exactly holding her against him. She sensed that he was already drawing back, gathering the emotions he had let slip earlier and locking them securely away.

Which, she thought, was probably a good idea considering the necessarily temporary nature of their personal relationship. She would be heading back to New York in a day or two—it was well past time for her to do so—and there was no purpose to be served by deluding themselves, even briefly, that there was anything more between them than a passionate attraction. Maybe it felt like more at the moment—maybe it felt like a *lot* more—but that was just her romanticizing things again. Fantasizing about a happy ending that was extremely unlikely.

She rubbed her cheek against Gideon's shoulder. "How are you feeling?"

"Pretty damned good," he answered without hesitation.

She laughed softly. "Glad to hear it."

He turned his head to look at her in the watery light that filtered in through the sheer curtains. She could just make out his faint smile. "That's what I call a full-service literary agency."

She smiled sweetly back at him and then punched him in the stomach.

Gideon laughed and caught her hand. The sound of his rare laughter made her breath catch.

So it felt a lot like love, she told herself wistfully. That didn't mean she had to get carried away by the fantasy.

"Sorry," he said, brushing a soft kiss against her knuckles. "Couldn't resist."

Though she knew he was talking about his lame joke,

her first thought was that she hadn't been able to resist him, either.

Still holding her wrist, he turned her hand over and pressed a kiss in her palm. Though she would have sworn that she was completely sated, she felt a renewed flicker of interest spark inside her in response to the feel of his warm lips against the sensitive skin of her palm. When he transferred his attentions to the hollow beneath her ear and then nibbled his way down the line of her jaw to the curve of her shoulder, the spark flared into a small flame. And when he slid a hand slowly down her quivering tummy to ease his fingertips into the nest of curls between her legs, the fire burned even hotter.

He moved against her hip, and she felt the unmistakable evidence that she wasn't the only one affected by the heat. "Oh, my."

His mouth was curved into a faint smile when he spoke against her lips. "Problem?"

"I'm just impressed by your stamina."

He nipped lightly at her lower lip. "You know what they say about writers."

"What—" She was forced to pause to clear her throat. "What do they say?"

"We keep working on a scene until we get it exactly right."

If he got it any more right this time, she was likely to explode, she decided, pressing her mouth to his as her arms went around him. But who was she to interfere with the creative process?

Chapter Twelve

Gideon didn't stay all night, whether because of Isabelle or for reasons of his own, Adrienne couldn't have said. He slipped out of bed as soon as he recovered his breath from their second round of lovemaking, donned his jeans and left her with a quick kiss on the cheek.

Though she half expected to lie awake the rest of the night, she fell deeply asleep almost the moment the bedroom door closed behind him. She slept without dreaming, waking to find the morning sun shining brightly through the windows.

A glance at the clock told her it was after eight. Isabelle was probably awake, since she shared her brother's predilection for early rising. Rolling slowly out of bed, Adrienne nearly stumbled when her feet tangled in the black nightgown lying discarded on the carpet. Glancing at the tumbled bedcovers, she groaned softly and pushed her hair out of her face. What had seemed like a good idea the night before looked different in the full light of day.

She didn't regret making love with Gideon, exactly. She just wasn't sure it had been wise to open herself up to heartache if she found she was unable to leave her growing feelings for him behind when she returned to her life in New York.

She took her time showering and dressing. When she finally went into the kitchen, she found Isabelle and Gideon sitting at the table, having breakfast. At least, Isabelle was eating cereal with sliced bananas. Gideon was reading the newspaper and drinking coffee—and from the look of the pot, it wasn't his first cup.

Pouring the remainder for herself, she carried her mug to the table, her chin held high as she greeted them brightly. Isabelle smiled and mumbled a return greeting around a mouthful of cereal. Gideon grunted and turned to the next page in the sports section.

So much for tender morning-after smiles, she thought wryly. "Aren't you having breakfast?"

"Not hungry. But help yourself."

"The cereal's good this morning," Isabelle said.

"Is it? Then I'll have that."

She fetched a bowl and filled it with cereal, milk and sliced bananas. Taking her seat, she spooned a bite into her mouth, chewed and swallowed, then nodded gravely to Isabelle. "You're right. The cereal is excellent this morning."

Gideon looked up from his newspaper. "I realized last night that I'm completely out of ink for my printer. I'm going to make an office supplies run this afternoon. It's about a forty-five-minute drive to the nearest office supplies warehouse. Will the two of you be okay here while I'm gone?"

He wasn't inviting them to join him. In fact, he seemed to be making a point to avoid doing so. Apparently, he needed some time to himself this afternoon. Because she knew him well enough by now to understand why, she nodded. ''We'll be fine.''

His gaze held hers a moment, no particular expression discernable in his eyes, and then he looked down at his paper again, the subject apparently settled.

Dipping her spoon into her bowl again, Adrienne wondered if this exasperating man would even remember her after she went away.

Gideon had been gone about an hour when the front doorbell rang. Because she wasn't expecting anyone, Adrienne glanced through the small window in the front door before turning the knob with a smile. ''If it isn't Officer Smith.''

He flashed his charmingly lazy smile. '''Afternoon, ma'am.''

''Gee, I know you're going to be terribly disappointed to hear this, but Gideon isn't here.''

''I know. I saw him driving out of town a while earlier. I figured this was as good a time as any to bring you this.''

This was a thick manila envelope, which he held out to her with the same rather sheepish expression he'd worn when he had told her about his writing.

''Your book?''

He nodded, swallowing visibly. ''You haven't changed your mind about wanting to read it?''

''Of course not. I'm delighted to read it.'' It was the absolute truth. She had become quite fond of Dylan Smith during the past few days, but more than that, she suspected that his book would be good.

And if it was? How would Gideon feel about her representing a man he was in the habit of despising? Would he consider it a conflict of interest, even though it would have absolutely no effect on her work for him?

She would worry about that after she read Dylan's book and decided whether it was worth representing.

"Come in," she said, holding the envelope and motioning with her free hand. "I'll make some coffee. You aren't on duty, are you?"

"Just went off. But I'd probably best not come in. Gideon—"

"Gideon told me to make myself at home during my visit," she interrupted firmly. "I'm sure that includes inviting my friends in for coffee. If it makes you feel any better, he'll be gone for another hour or so, so you won't have to see him."

"Something tells me he wouldn't agree with you about inviting me in. He's more likely to blow a gasket." But he entered, anyway, looking around as if checking to make sure Gideon wasn't lurking somewhere inside.

"Officer Smith!" Isabelle ran toward him with her arms outstretched.

He swung her into the air, making her squeal with delight. "How's the little princess?"

Her sneakered feet pumping the air, Isabelle giggled. "Princess Isabelle. I like that."

"So do I." He lowered her to the floor. "Whatcha' been up to since yesterday?"

"Adrienne and I went outside and played hopscotch. She's good. But I'm better."

Dylan laughed and winked at Adrienne. "Well, you *are* Princess Isabelle."

Adrienne led him into the kitchen and motioned him into a chair while she put the coffee on. While it brewed, Isabelle entertained them with a song and dance she had learned at school. Leaving Dylan laughing, she dashed into the other room to draw him a picture to take with him when he left.

"That kid's cute, isn't she?"

Smiling in response to his indulgent tone, Adrienne opened the cabinet where Gideon kept the sugar and powdered creamer. "I'm crazy about her."

"Gideon seems rather fond of her, too."

Hearing the undertone of surprise in his voice, she looked at him over her shoulder. "He is. He's not one to express his feelings very easily, but he has grown quite close to his little sister during this past week."

"I'm glad the family has been able to accept the kid," Dylan said in a low voice. "It couldn't have been easy for Lenore and Gideon, considering Isabelle's parents were Lenore's husband and Gideon's girlfriend, but it's a good thing they don't blame the little girl for her parents—are you okay?"

Adrienne stared dumbly down at the shards of broken mug scattered around her feet. She would have to replace that before she left. It seemed to have leaped out of her hand. "I'm fine. Just clumsy."

"I didn't give anything away, did I? I mean, the way everyone gossips in this town, I figured you knew…"

"Gideon's told me a bit about his family history." With the exception of a few pertinent details, of course.

Dylan made a sound of self-disgust and shook his head. "I have a habit of opening my mouth and inserting my foot. I didn't mean to come into Gideon's kitchen and start gossiping about his family. I was just trying to say that I'm glad that sweet little orphan girl ended up with a family who cares about her, despite the past."

"So am I." Having cleaned up her breakage, she set his coffee cup in front of him and settled on the other side of the table with her own. "Tell me more about your book, Dylan. You said you envision it as the first in a series?"

He followed her lead with an eagerness that proved he was grateful for the change of subject.

Within minutes they had moved from his writing to other books they both enjoyed and from that to films and music. Adrienne liked Dylan very much, and she had a healthy feminine appreciation for his cowboy charm, but there was no real chemistry between them at all. It was like having coffee with her favorite male cousin. And even though Dylan flirted with her a bit—a knee-jerk, guy thing, most likely—she sensed that he felt much the same way about her.

Dylan's smile faded quickly when the front doorbell rang. "Great. That's probably Gideon. I'm telling you, Adrienne, he isn't going to like this."

"Gideon wouldn't ring his own doorbell. He parks in the garage and comes in through the kitchen. I'll go see who it is."

Peering through the door window, she didn't recognize the attractive and ridiculously happy couple on the doorstep, but she thought she could make a guess at their identity. She opened the door, but before she could speak, she was interrupted by a high-pitched squeal from behind her.

"Nate!" Isabelle shot forward, bouncing with excitement. "You're home!"

"Hi, poppet." The golden-haired, blue-eyed man snatched her up in his arms, raining half a dozen kisses on her cheeks, which made her squirm and giggle. "How's my girl?"

Isabelle responded with a rush of tangled words.

The brown-haired woman who had followed Nathan inside gave Adrienne a rueful smile. "Please forgive our rudeness in barging in this way. I'm Nathan's wife, Caitlin, as you've probably figured out. You must be Gideon's agent.''

''Adrienne Corley.'' She shook the other woman's hand warmly, pleased to have this chance to meet Isabelle's guardians. ''But I thought you weren't returning for another week.''

''To be honest we were both anxious to come home. With Lenore's sister injured and poor Gideon trying to finish his book, we decided we were needed here. And, as spectacular as our honeymoon was, we missed Isabelle.''

Glancing at Nathan and Isabelle, Adrienne realized that Gideon hadn't exaggerated about the strength of the bond between this new family. It appeared that Isabelle would be raised with all the love and attention a child could ask for.

''Gideon isn't here right now. He had to go to an office supplies store.''

Settling Isabelle on his hip, Nathan smiled at Adrienne. ''Then we won't expect him anytime soon. Gideon feels about office supplies stores the way most men do about hardware stores. He can spend hours in them looking at organizers and notebooks and pens and computer accessories.''

Though the image of Gideon as a serious shopper was rather odd to her, Adrienne said only, ''Would either of you like a cup of coffee? I have a fresh pot in the kitchen.''

Nathan's blue eyes lit up eagerly. ''Coffee sounds great. And do you suppose Gideon's got the makings for a sandwich in there? We've been traveling all day and I'm about wiped out.''

''Nathan,'' his bride protested, ''you can't just barge into your brother's house and raid his refrigerator.''

He flashed her a grin. ''Watch me.''

''I'm sure Gideon wouldn't mind,'' Adrienne said,

though it occurred to her that she'd been awfully free with Gideon's hospitality that day.

She happened to be watching Nathan's face when he saw Dylan sitting at Gideon's table drinking coffee. Until that moment she had seen little resemblance between the McCloud brothers, but Nathan's expression reminded her very much of Gideon.

"What the hell are you doing here?"

"Nate." Clucking her tongue reprovingly, Isabelle tapped her brother's shoulder. "That's not very nice."

His smile looking quite different from the one he'd worn earlier, Dylan stood. "That's okay, Princess Isabelle. I'm used to it from your brothers."

"That doesn't make it any more acceptable." Caitlin frowned at Nathan, then held out her hand to Dylan. "It's nice to see you, Officer Smith."

"You, too, ma'am." He shook her hand, his expression marginally warmer than it had been when he'd faced her husband. "And congratulations on your marriage."

She laughed. "Even if I *did* marry a McCloud? Never mind, I know what your answer to that would be."

He only smiled.

Adrienne felt the need to defend Dylan's presence. "Dylan has been quite gracious to me during my visit here. He was very helpful to me and Isabelle when we were involved in the minor car accident on Tuesday, and he—"

"A car accident?" Frowning, Nathan looked at Isabelle again as if searching for overlooked injuries. "Why didn't I hear about that?"

"I thought Gideon had mentioned it to you to explain why I've been staying here. I guess he didn't want to alarm you, especially since no one was hurt. Officer Smith arrived at the scene almost immediately, and he took excellent care of Isabelle and me when I carelessly fell and sprained my ankle.''

Caitlin nodded. ''I did notice that you were limping.''

''What happened?'' Nathan asked, still looking concerned.

''A red sports car ran a red light in front of me, causing me to slam on my brakes and go into a spin on wet pavement. The back of my car hit a lamppost, but Isabelle and I were both securely strapped in, so we weren't harmed.''

''A red sports car.'' Nathan gave Dylan a look. ''Did you get him?''

''I didn't have positive ID. Adrienne couldn't describe the car.''

''It happened too fast,'' Adrienne added, somewhat apologetically.

Nathan was still looking at Dylan. ''Did you talk to Sawyer?''

''Yeah. He denied even being in his car that day.''

Nathan made a sound of disgust. ''Of course he did.''

His eyebrows rising, Dylan asked, ''Isn't this your own client you're talking about?''

''Not anymore. I suggested after his last DUI that he seek another attorney. For his sake it should probably be someone who doesn't want to see him thrown into jail.''

Dylan chuckled.

Taking encouragement from that very brief accord, Adrienne said, ''I'll start preparing the sandwiches. Caitlin, would you mind making a fresh pot of coffee?''

''I'd be happy to,'' she said, then gave Dylan a smile. ''You might as well join us. As often as we encounter each other professionally—even on opposite sides, occasionally—it's ridiculous to pretend we're total strangers.''

Both Nathan and Dylan looked dubious.

"Attorneys and cops are rarely bosom buddies," Nathan explained.

"Not to mention my personal history with the Mc-Clouds," Dylan added.

"Then we'll agree not to talk about work or past grievances," Adrienne said firmly. "Trust me, I've had very pleasant meals at tables with authors, agents, editors and publishing executives. If a disparate group like that can put aside their professional conflicts for a few hours, I'm sure you two can. You grew up in the same small town, for heaven's sake. You must have some mutual friends or root for the same sports teams—*something* in common."

"What we have in common is a long history of mutual dislike," Nathan muttered.

"Well, *I* like you both," Isabelle asserted firmly. "And I think you should be friends."

After a moment of silence, Caitlin laughed.

"A decree from Princess Isabelle," Dylan said, his smile wry. "I suppose we can make an effort to be sociable—for an hour or so."

"Well, glory be." Caitlin grinned as she moved toward the coffeemaker. "Maybe there's hope for world peace, after all."

"Not if Gideon walks in anytime soon," Nathan predicted glumly, setting Isabelle on her feet. "World War III's gonna break out right here in this kitchen if he walks in and finds us helping ourselves to his food and sharing it with Smith."

"I'll make Gideon behave," Isabelle promised confidently, making the adults laugh again.

While Adrienne wouldn't have said Nathan and Dylan were friendly, exactly, as they dined on ham and cheese sandwiches with chips and pickle spears, they were at least civil. Yet both made a point of addressing their comments to either her, Caitlin or Isabelle, and rarely to each other.

Though it was, of course, absolutely none of her business, she was still very curious about what had gone wrong between Dylan Smith and Deborah McCloud—and why it had left such hard feelings in her brothers. Adrienne was also intensely curiously about Dylan's offhand comment about Isabelle's mother being Gideon's girlfriend.

Was that the primary cause of his lingering antipathy toward his late father? Had he loved her? Did he see her face every time he looked at Isabelle?

Darn it, why hadn't he said anything to her? As much as she told herself he had been under no obligation whatsoever to tell her anything about his past, she was still irrationally angry with him for not doing so.

Perhaps because the omission reminded her so graphically that he only saw her as a temporary diversion in his life.

Gideon heard the sounds as soon as he stepped out of his truck and into his garage. Voices, laughter, the muted clatter of dishware—was there a damned party going on in his kitchen?

His hands filled with bags from the office warehouse, he stalked toward the kitchen door. He froze in the doorway when he saw the group gathered around his table. He was surprised to see Nathan and Caitlin, of course, since he hadn't expected them for another week. But he was absolutely flabbergasted to see Dylan Smith sitting there with them.

Last he'd heard, which hadn't been that long ago, Nathan hadn't been any fonder of Smith than Gideon was. Now he was sitting here having afternoon tea with the guy?

Apparently, the group had been laughing at something cute that Isabelle had said and hadn't heard him open the door. Caitlin was the one who spotted him first. "Red alert," she said comically.

Everyone looked around at him, their smiles fading.

Isabelle made a stern face and wagged a finger at him. "Now, Gideon. Be nice."

Dylan pushed himself to his feet. "I think I'd better be going. I, uh, have to do some laundry."

"Freeze, Smith." Gideon set his purchases on a counter. "What the—" Catching a glimpse of Isabelle, he changed his words. "What's going on?"

Adrienne seemed to be the designated explainer. "Nathan and Caitlin decided to spend the rest of their honeymoon with Isabelle. Dylan dropped by to bring me something I had requested from him. We've been having a nice visit over coffee and sandwiches. Would you like something to eat?"

How graciously she had offered him his own food, he thought with a scowl. "No."

"Coffee?"

"No."

Dylan had taken another couple of steps toward the doorway. "I really think it would be best if I just go."

Gideon shot him a look. "Damn straight. And I'd better not find you in my house again."

Though the other man had obviously been trying to avoid a confrontation, he stiffened in response to Gideon's surly challenge, his male ego piqued. "Trust me, I have no desire to pay any social calls on you."

Isabelle poked out her lower lip. "You can come visit me at Nate's house, Officer Smith," she said, giving Gideon a reproachful look. "Nate will be nice if I ask him to."

Now *everyone* was looking at Gideon as though he were the killjoy who had arrived to ruin their pleasant afternoon. Even Nathan looked more concerned with Isabelle's displeasure than sympathetic with Gideon's plight at finding an old enemy at his table. He'd never expected his own family to take Dylan Smith's side over his.

Dylan patted her cheek. "Thank you, princess Isabelle. I'm sure I'll see you around town. I'll make a point to stop and visit with you when I do, okay?"

She seemed only partially appeased.

Glancing at Adrienne with an I-warned-you expression that even Gideon could read, Dylan asked, "When will you be heading back to New York?"

"Tomorrow. I'll call you. You did leave me your number, didn't you?"

"It's in the package. Have a safe trip back."

He left a heavy silence behind him when he departed without another glance at Gideon.

"Well," Nathan said after a beat. "That was fun."

Still itching to fight—especially after that cozy exchange between Dylan and Adrienne—Gideon rounded on his brother. "I shouldn't have had to throw him out. You should have already taken care of that."

Her dark eyes glinting dangerously, Adrienne stepped toward him. "Isabelle, sweetie, why don't you show Caitlin the pictures you've drawn at school this week? They're in your room."

Caitlin eagerly seized the chance to escape the impending confrontation. "I would love to see your schoolwork, Isabelle. And I want to hear all about your week."

Still sending Gideon a look that gave him the urge to shuffle his feet on the floor like a schoolboy in trouble with his parents, Isabelle took Caitlin's hand and left the room.

"Now," Adrienne said when she, Nathan and Gideon were alone in the kitchen. "Why don't you vent your bad temper at the person who is responsible, rather than innocent bystanders? *I* invited Dylan into this house because he has become a friend of mine. I knew you wouldn't particularly like it, but I didn't think you would be quite so rude and ungracious about it."

"It wasn't all Adrienne's fault," Nathan supplied gallantly. "I'm the one who suggested raiding your refrigerator. Caitlin invited Dylan to join us for a sandwich. So you might as well be mad at all of us."

"Trust me, I am."

Nathan nodded. "Fair enough."

"I just can't understand why you'd suddenly be all cozy with Smith," Gideon complained, shoving a hand through his hair. "I know we've nicknamed you Nathan the Peacemaker, but you've always disliked that guy as much as I have."

"What makes you think I've suddenly changed my mind about him? I haven't, and he made no pretense to be any more fond of me. We agreed to be civil for a couple of hours for Adrienne's sake and for Isabelle's."

Something he, of course, had failed to do. Torn between self-righteous indignation and an uncharacteristic ripple of guilt, Gideon glanced at his still-angry agent. "I didn't like finding him in my house."

"You've made that perfectly clear," she snapped, and he almost winced in response to her sharp-edged tone. "I apologize for my breach of etiquette, and I can assure you it won't happen again. For one thing, I'll be leaving tomorrow, and I doubt I'll ever be in a position to invite anyone inside your house again."

Nathan cleared his throat. "I think I'll go look at Isabelle's drawings."

Ignoring his departing brother, Gideon concentrated on Adrienne, instead. "When did you decide to go back tomorrow?"

Her voice was cool when she replied. "That's pretty much been a given all along, hasn't it? You asked me to stay for the weekend so I would have a chance to attend the festival. Now that your brother and sister-in-law have returned to collect Isabelle, there's no reason for me to stay."

No reason at all why she should, he silently agreed—except that, no matter how annoyed he was that she'd brought Dylan Smith into his home, he still wasn't ready for her to leave. It would have been nice to have a chance to spend more time alone with her, now that they wouldn't be baby-sitting.

He supposed he had pretty much blown any chance of a replay of last night's spectacular lovemaking.

Those intimate hours had replayed themselves over and over in his mind all day. He had needed to get away for a few hours to put the interlude into perspective. The emotions between them had flared uncomfortably high last night, but he'd convinced himself that there was no reason to be worried that either of them would be hurt. He and Adrienne were hardly inexperienced kids; they both knew the score and were both prepared to say goodbye when the time came to do so.

He just hadn't realized the time was quite so close.

"Look," he said, shaking his head in self-disgust, "I know you don't understand the history between Dylan Smith and me. And I know you like the guy, for some reason I can't imagine. What I'm trying to say is, I'm not really angry with you for inviting Smith in, even though he should have known better than to accept."

"How very gracious of you." The ice dripping from her words made his skin chill.

He had definitely blown his chance for another night of passion.

"Gideon?" Caitlin stood in the kitchen doorway, looking uncertainly from him to Adrienne. "Nathan and I are tired, and we'd like to get home. I've got Isabelle's things packed and she's waiting in the living room to say goodbye."

"You're leaving now?"

She nodded. "I'm sure you'll be glad to get back to your usual routines without worrying about keeping an eye on Isabelle."

Since that was exactly the way he *should* feel, he couldn't imagine why he suddenly felt his scowl deepening. "I'll come see her off. Adrienne?"

"Yes, I'd like to say goodbye to her."

Isabelle waited in the living room with Nathan. Her big red suitcase and purple backpack sat by the door, and she held her white owl in one hand. Her expression was grave when she looked at Gideon, and he suspected she was still annoyed with him for being mean, in her opinion, to her friend Dylan.

He swallowed a sigh and knelt in front of her. "I'm sorry I came home grouchy."

She looked at him through her lashes. "You made Dylan leave."

"Isabelle, you know Dylan and I aren't friends. It has nothing to do with you or the way you feel about either of us."

"You're making Adrienne leave, too. She said she's going away tomorrow."

He shook his head. "Adrienne knows she's welcome to stay here as long as she likes. But she was only here for a visit—like you were. And now she needs to go home—like you do.''

''Then you'll be here all by yourself. Won't you be lonely?''

Gideon was relieved when Nathan answered for him. ''Gideon likes living by himself, poppet. It's easier for him to write his books that way.''

''Sometimes he forgets to eat. Adrienne makes him stop working so he won't get too hungry.''

It occurred to Gideon only then that his little sister was actually worried about him, even if she was still rather irritated with him. ''I won't forget to eat,'' he promised. ''When I get hungry, I'll eat. I've been taking care of myself for a long time.''

''But what if you get lonely?''

''Then I'll pick up the phone and give you a call,'' he answered with a smile. ''Maybe you can go have ice cream with me sometime. Okay?''

She thought about that a moment, then nodded. ''Okay.''

And then she wrapped her arms around his neck and gave him a smacking kiss on the cheek. ''Thank you for letting me stay with you, Gideon.''

She still had a unique way of saying his name, he thought with an odd lump in his throat. He was going to miss hearing it.

He stood to one side and watched as Isabelle and Adrienne said their goodbyes with hugs and kisses.

''When will I see you again?'' Isabelle asked.

''I don't know when I'll be back,'' Adrienne answered evasively. ''But I won't forget you, sweetie. And I'll always treasure the picture you drew for me.''

Nathan swung Isabelle into his arms. ''I'll call you,'' he

said to Gideon. "And thanks for helping out with Isabelle."

Gideon nodded. "I enjoyed it," he said, and realized that it was the truth, for the most part.

Nathan's family departed in a final rush of words and noise that made the silence all the more noticeable when the door closed behind them. Pushing his hands into his pockets, Gideon looked at Adrienne, thinking of the other goodbye that faced them.

She was probably more than ready to get back to her real life, especially after today. But, damn it, as much as it galled him to admit it, it wasn't going to be easy for him to let her go.

Chapter Thirteen

As ridiculous as it was to think of a four-year-old as a chaperone, Adrienne was intensely aware of being alone with Gideon. She certainly had no fear of him, not after spending the past week with him, even in his worst moods.

Gideon, she had decided, was like one of those quiet little dogs that growled when they felt threatened. For some reason her friendship with Dylan bothered him enough to make him growl.

Understanding his bad behavior did not, of course, excuse it.

Straightening her shoulders, she adopted a briskly professional manner when she turned back to him. "I'll need to make some travel arrangements this afternoon—airline reservations, transportation to the airport—"

"I'll take you to the airport," he broke in to say.

She nodded. "Thank you. Since I'll probably need to leave early tomorrow, I suggest we spend the rest of today talking business. I need your decision on several options, and we need to discuss what I should say to your editor when I talk to her next. If you think you'll need more time for your current book, I'll arrange for an extension on your deadline so we won't have any contractual problems."

He nodded. "Fine. Let's go to my office and talk business. I'd hate for you to leave feeling like you wasted a trip."

She certainly didn't feel as though the time had been wasted, she mused, following him to his office. But she wouldn't know until later whether it had been a big mistake.

That all depended on how long it took her to get over the foolish infatuation she had developed for this thoroughly exasperating man.

They talked about business for two full hours, Adrienne making copious notes as Gideon efficiently dispensed with the pending matters. She didn't agree with all his decisions, and she felt it was her job to give her opinions. But in the end his wishes prevailed.

Satisfied that they had accomplished all they could, Adrienne packed away her papers. "I suppose that takes care of everything until after I speak with your editor next week."

"Everything business related," he agreed, moving toward her.

She took a half step backward. "I should start packing my—"

Her words faded when his hands fell on her shoulders. "We've gotten our business out of the way, but we still have some personal issues we need to discuss."

She made herself meet his eyes. "What personal issues?"

"Well, for starters, there's *this*." He pressed his mouth to hers.

Her hands rested on his chest when he finally lifted his head. "There is that," she agreed huskily.

"You're not still mad at me?"

"I was never—" She stopped, then made a face. "Okay, I was annoyed with you earlier. But this is your home and I had no right to invite someone in when I knew you wouldn't approve. You had every right to be angry."

"Okay, we've both apologized for anything we might have done wrong. Can we put it behind us now?"

She motioned toward the desk and the neat stack of paperwork they had worked on together. "I thought we'd already done that."

He nodded. "Professionally, of course. I have no doubt we'll work together as well as we ever did. But I don't want to spend our last night together talking business or glowering at each other."

"I don't want that, either."

"So how about if we go out? We've spent the past week sitting here in the house with Isabelle. We deserve an adult night out, don't you think?"

Even though she suspected she was just asking for more achingly bittersweet memories, she nodded. "I'd like that."

"Okay, then." He stepped back. "I guess I'd better change."

"Yes, so will I."

"By the way," he said as they parted in the hallway outside the office. "I bought an answering machine while I was out. I'll hook it up before you leave tomorrow."

"That should make things much easier for people who need to reach you."

He shrugged. "I suppose. But then, if I'd had it sooner, you wouldn't have felt the need to come here."

She smiled at him. "No, I suppose not."

Clearing his throat, he glanced away. "Let me get my clothes for tonight out of my room, and I'll change in the bathroom."

"I guess you'll be glad to have your own room back—not to mention the rest of your house."

His expression impossible to read, he turned and walked away without answering.

Adrienne had known, of course, that Gideon could be quite charming when he chose to be. She had seen flashes of that charm during the past few days, but that night he went to great lengths to make sure she had a pleasant time.

They dined at a very nice Italian restaurant, far different from the smoky diner where he'd treated her to breakfast earlier that week. Gideon looked incredibly handsome in a dark suit, a crisp white shirt and a red tie, his longish dark hair neatly brushed away from his face. She had a feeling he didn't bother to dress up very often, and she was flattered that he'd chosen to do so tonight, for her.

As much as he might pretend to be a socially awkward loner, this was a man who was perfectly comfortable in an upscale restaurant. He might claim to be the wet blanket at parties, but that was only because he chose to be, not because he didn't know better. Aware now of his family background—that his father had been a successful business leader who had held several local offices before his aborted run for governor—she knew Gideon must have been trained in etiquette from childhood. That training was very much in evidence during their dinner.

She had no doubt that he could handle any situation he might encounter during a book tour or any other promotional opportunity she might convince him to accept. *If* she could convince him, of course.

"Tell me more about your life in New York," he said over their entrees. "What's a typical day like for you?"

He was even making small talk. The guy was going all-out.

"I'm in my office by eight so I can work for an hour or so before the phones start ringing at nine. I'm on the phone until noon, I usually have lunch meetings scheduled, and take phone calls again in the afternoons. I leave the office at six, usually have an evening meeting of some sort, then get home by ten and work on paperwork until midnight, at which time I fall facefirst into bed until six the next morning."

"And on weekends?"

"I do my shopping, read manuscripts and contracts, maybe attend a few professional social functions or an occasional dinner party with friends. On the second Sunday of every month, I have brunch with my father and his latest young bride."

He skillfully twirled linguine onto a fork. "And you're happy with this life?"

She shrugged. "I'm not unhappy."

"Doesn't sound very exciting."

She lifted an eyebrow. "And your life is a thrill a minute? Remember, I've spent the past week with you, and I know your daily routine. You wake up early, hit the computer, stop to eat when you think about it, do a little housework every afternoon while you work out the next scene and then you write again until you fall asleep—sometimes on the couch in your office."

He looked disgruntled. "You think you know me so well, do you?"

"Are you saying I'm wrong?"

He filled his mouth with a bite of bread to avoid answering—which, of course, was an answer in itself.

So neither of them were exactly party animals, she mused, stabbing a slice of steamed zucchini. What was wrong with that?

Washing the bread down with a sip of water, he set his glass down before asking, "How many times has your father been married?"

"Four. No, three. I don't think he and Louisa were ever actually married. Louisa was the young blond who moved in after my mother died," she added.

"You said you were twelve when you lost your mother?"

She wasn't surprised that he had remembered; not much escaped Gideon. "Yes."

"Were your parents still married then?"

"Yes. As far as I know, my father was a faithful, if obsessively workaholic, husband. My mother's illness was brief, and I think he grieved for her, in his own way, before he started dating Louisa a few months later. In the past sixteen years, none of his other relationships have lasted more than a couple of years. Some people think it's because no other woman can compare to the memories of my mother."

"And what do you think?"

"I think no other woman since my mother has been willing to put up with his cool, distant, controlling and completely self-absorbed nature."

"And this is the man you've spent your whole life trying to please?"

"Pretty much."

He sat in silence for a moment, then shrugged. "Your choice, I guess."

"Yes. It is."

Nodding toward their hovering server, he asked, "Would you like some dessert?"

The conversation about her father was over before she could figure out a way to ask a few questions about his relationship with his own father—and his father's second wife. Questions she had no right to ask, of course, but that had been driving her crazy all day.

Gideon's house was very quiet when they reentered it later that evening. They had been talking about something inconsequential during the drive home from the restaurant, but they both fell silent when they entered his empty kitchen and spotted a little purple plastic bracelet lying forgotten on the table.

"You'll miss her, won't you?" she asked, studying Gideon's face as he looked at the bracelet.

He shrugged and set his truck keys on the counter. "I can see her whenever I want. Take her out for ice cream or something."

"That's not quite the same."

"Are you kidding? It's better this way." He took a glass down from a cabinet and filled it with tap water. "I can spend an hour or two with her, then turn her back over to Nathan and Caitlin when she gets bored or tired. I don't have to worry about dentist or doctor appointments, or whether she's done her homework every night, or whether she bathes or brushes or eats her veggies—all the day-to-day minutiae of child-rearing."

He tilted his head back to drink the water and she watched his throat work as he swallowed. Everything about him was attractive to her. She wanted to press her lips to the pulse in his throat, taste the skin over his sexy Adam's apple.

Did he feel much the same way about her that he did about Isabelle? He enjoyed being with her while she was here, but would it be nice when he didn't have to worry if she was entertained or hungry or annoyed—what he would probably call the day-to-day minutiae of a relationship?

Maybe she should look at it that way, too. After all, Gideon was a very difficult man. Living with him on a daily basis would be challenging, to say the least. She should take full advantage of the few hours she had left with him and then walk away with a heart full of fond memories and a sense of relief that she didn't have to deal with his capricious moods any longer.

That was exactly the way she *should* feel, she just wasn't sure that she would.

Setting the empty glass down, he turned to her, his heavy-lidded green eyes somber on her face. "I suppose you're tired."

It wasn't a question, but a question lay behind it. Only a few more hours, she reminded herself, and moved toward him. "No," she said, sliding her hands up his chest. "I'm not tired."

He caught her wrists, holding both her hands in front of him. For just a moment she thought he was going to decline her implicit invitation, and she wondered why. Was he still annoyed with her for inviting Dylan inside? Had he already mentally said his goodbyes?

But then he lifted her hands to brush his lips across her knuckles. "Did I tell you how pretty you look tonight?"

She melted, of course. How could such a simple line— one she had heard so many times before—affect her so deeply when Gideon said it? Heaven only knew how she would react if he started spouting poetry. "Thank you."

Still holding her gaze with his, he dropped her hands, then swung her into his arms without warning. She gave a laughing gasp and clutched at his shoulders. "Gideon," she said, her legs dangling over his arm.

Flashing one of his rare, wicked grins, he turned toward the kitchen doorway. "I'm only thinking of your injured ankle," he assured her, striding confidently down the hallway toward his bedroom. "You should probably keep your weight off it for the rest of the evening."

"That's very considerate of you," she said with as much dignity as possible.

"You could probably use a good massage, too. I've been told I have very talented hands."

She eyed him speculatively. "I won't ask how many people have told you that."

"A very select few," he assured her, lowering her to his bed.

The thought of Isabelle's mother flashed very briefly through her mind, but she pushed it away. His past was none of her business. Neither was his future, for that matter, except where it concerned his writing. All they had was tonight, and she would be foolish to waste a minute of it.

She reached for the top button of her blouse. "Massages feel best against bare skin, I understand."

His tie was already off, and he tossed his jacket over the back of a nearby chair. "Most definitely."

"But I thought it was only the client who disrobes, not the masseur."

His hands fell to his belt buckle. "I have my own way of doing things."

"You can say that again."

Shedding the last of his clothes, he loomed over her. "Roll over."

She still wore her black bra and panties. For some reason—perhaps the way he was looking at her just then—

she felt more vulnerable in those expensive scraps of lace than if she had been completely nude.

He very efficiently flipped her onto her tummy.

She jumped a little when his hands fell on her shoulders.

"Relax," he said. "You're too stiff."

She moved just a little, brushing against him with her hip. "You're one to talk."

"Be still," he said, just a hint of amusement in his voice as his fingers made short work of the back fastening of her bra. And then he went to work on her knotted muscles.

Those other select people, who she would rather not think about, had been entirely correct, she mused with a sound that was a cross between a moan and a purr. Gideon had *very* talented hands.

They had been sharing a very quiet breakfast the next morning when Gideon noticed the manila envelope on the counter near the coffeemaker. "What's this?" he asked, picking it up. "Something you forgot to pack?"

Adrienne still looked a bit heavy-eyed from their near-sleepless night. They hadn't wanted to waste a moment of their remaining time together.

"Yes," she said, glancing at the envelope without elaborating.

He scowled when he saw Dylan Smith's name, address and telephone number printed neatly on the outside of the envelope. "This is the reason Smith was here yesterday? Was is it, a copy of your accident report?"

But no, he thought, it was much too thick for anything like that. It felt very much like a manuscript—but surely not.

"It's just something I wanted to see," she answered evasively. "I'll stick it in my briefcase."

He handed her the envelope. "So what's Smith done, written a book?"

He had spoken lightly, not really believing it, but the expression that crossed Adrienne's face made him stiffen. "Oh, hell," he muttered. "Tell me I'm wrong."

"The contents of this envelope are between Dylan and me," she told him, avoiding his eyes. "I don't think he would appreciate it if I discussed his business with you."

It wasn't his business, of course. She had no obligation at all to discuss anything with him, despite the past two nights. But just the thought of her having secrets with Dylan Smith was enough to make Gideon see red.

"Surely that guy isn't trying to call himself a writer these days. And even if he is, you wouldn't seriously consider representing him."

Her eyebrows rose. "That would be my decision, wouldn't it?"

"There is such a thing as a professional conflict of interest."

"And this isn't it," she shot back. "You are not my only client, Gideon. You know that. I've never once neglected you for any of the others. In fact, I would say I've gone rather above the call of duty on your behalf."

Thinking of the things they had shared during the past week, he glowered. "I damn well hope you don't treat all your clients exactly the same."

She rose very slowly to her feet, her eyes narrowing with the temper he had seen from her only once before. "I have never slept with another client, if that's what you're referring to. It isn't something I plan to make a habit of. And you know very well that my decision to do so with you had nothing to do with business."

Hearing a hint of hurt beneath the anger, he grimaced. "Look, I didn't mean it that way—"

"That's certainly the way it sounded. And I didn't appreciate it."

"Adrienne, I'm sorry. It's just, well, you know how I get about Dylan Smith."

"Yes, I know how you get about him. And to be honest, I'm fed up with it. At least Dylan makes an effort to be civil, despite your macho posturing around each other."

Her defense of Dylan piqued his own temper all over again. "Then I guess you'll be glad to get back to New York and away from my uncivilized behavior," he said stiffly.

"I certainly *should* be glad," she snapped.

Because she hadn't actually said she *would* be glad, he was somewhat appeased. Giving a disgruntled look at the envelope that had started this quarrel—and thinking that Dylan could cause trouble even when he wasn't around—he told himself he should let it go. Even if Dylan Smith did have delusions of following in Gideon's creative footsteps, it didn't mean the guy actually had talent. The book was probably a poor imitation of Gideon's books, and Adrienne was too professional to pretend otherwise, no matter how much she liked the jerk.

"I'm sorry," he repeated. "You're right. It's none of my business."

She moved her head in a barely perceptible nod. "I'll go make sure I have all of my things out of your room. We have to leave soon."

He swallowed a curse as he watched her stalk out of the room. Seemed like every time he turned around he ticked her off.

It was probably a good thing that she was leaving now, before he made her so angry she would never speak to him again. He was lousy with relationships—even the temporary kind. Just as well this one was over, he assured himself, trying to ignore the hollow feeling deep inside him.

Gideon walked her as far as the check-in counter at the airport. They hadn't said much during the drive, though Adrienne had made an effort to put their spat behind them and get back to a professional tone with him. She could stew about her pain and irritation with him during the long flight home.

"There's no need for you to hang around," she told him. "You've got a long drive back, and I'll have to sit around here for a while."

Pushing his hands in his pockets, he nodded. "I guess I'll go, then. You're sure you'll be okay? Your ankle's not bothering you?"

"It's still sore, of course, but I'll sit whenever I have the chance. I won't overdo it." She had worn her sock-and-brace again, leaving the crutches behind for Gideon to return to the doctor. She figured she would be tired and sore by the time she finally reached her apartment that evening, but she would make it.

"You'll ask for help if you need it?"

"Of course I will," she answered heartily, but she knew she lied. She was too accustomed to looking after herself.

He didn't look particularly reassured by her answer, but he only nodded again.

She shifted her purse more comfortably on her shoulder, clutching her bulging briefcase in her hands. "I'll call you in a few days—after I talk to your editor."

"I'll try to have the book finished in a couple of weeks."

She hesitated, then took the risk of annoying him again. "You haven't considered changing the ending?"

"It's moving along fine the way I planned it."

She studied his mulish expression for a moment, then sighed and shook her head. "Stubborn man."

His slight smile was rueful. "Bossy woman."

She chuckled and spoke without thinking. "Quite a pair, aren't we?"

He reached up to touch her cheek in a gesture that was uncharacteristically sweet, coming from him. "We certainly were."

His use of the past tense made her smile fade. "Well," she said, gripping her things more tightly, "I guess I'd better get started with all the security checks."

"Yes, that does take a while. So, goodbye, then."

Feeling a bit foolish, she stuck out her right hand. "Goodbye."

He glanced at her hand, scowled, then reached out to snag the back of her neck and pull her toward him. He kissed her firmly, with the arrogant possessiveness that was entirely characteristic of him. Only when he had kissed her half-senseless did he release her, stepping back so abruptly she staggered a little.

"Take care of yourself," he said, his voice gruff.

And then he was gone.

Despite her best intentions, Adrienne found herself wiping tears as she turned toward the counter.

Chapter Fourteen

"Gideon, I want you to come to lunch. Your brother and sisters will be disappointed if you aren't here—especially Isabelle."

The telephone propped in the crook of his shoulder, his hands on his keyboard, Gideon answered rather impatiently, "I really can't come tomorrow, Mom. You know I'm trying to finish this book."

"Yes, and I know that you have to take a little time off to eat. We won't expect you to stay long, but no one has seen you in weeks."

"It hasn't been that long. You've only been home from Aunt Wanda's a week." And Adrienne had been gone for three weeks, he added silently. Yet with all the solitude and freedom to write he'd had since, he still hadn't finished this damned book.

"And I haven't laid eyes on you since I got back. Are you sure you're okay?"

"I'm fine, Mom. Just busy."

"Not too busy to eat. I'll expect you at twelve-thirty tomorrow."

"Mom, I—"

"And don't be late. The rest of us will be hungry."

His next protest was met only by the sound of a dial tone.

Slamming the telephone back into the receiver, he muttered a string of phrases he couldn't have said if Isabelle had been there. Not that it did any good. He knew very well he would be at his mother's for lunch the next day, whether he was in the mood or not.

"So then I informed him that if he wants to continue to publish Stephen's books under his imprint, he's going to have to make it worth our while. I expect a new offer on my desk by tomorrow afternoon."

The smug satisfaction in Lawrence Corley's voice was extremely familiar to his daughter; she had been hearing it all her life. She couldn't remember him ever actually admitting that he had failed or handled any situation in a less than brilliant manner.

There had been a time when she'd thought she had to compete with her father's idea of perfection. Now she simply acknowledged it. "That's great, Dad. I'm sure Stephen will be pleased with you, as always."

"Everyone knows Stephen is lucky to have Lawrence as his agent," Melinda Corley, Lawrence's thirty-year-old bride, murmured. The lights of the popular Sunday-brunch restaurant gleamed attractively on her perfectly blond tresses and illuminated the perfection of her buffed-bronzed-and-botoxed skin. "Lawrence is the best literary agent in the business."

Keeping her smile bright and bland, Adrienne stabbed

her fork into a chunk of fresh mango. "The rest of us can only aspire to be half as good."

"By the way," Lawrence said as if her statement had been a given that didn't require a response, "has Gideon McCloud finished that book yet?"

She kept her eyes focused on the sparsely-filled plate on the table in front of her. "Not as far as I know."

Her father pointed a spear of broccoli at her. "That young man is going to derail his career just as it's getting into high gear, if he isn't careful. Maybe I need to—"

"I can handle my own clients, Dad."

"Not if you keep taking those long vacations," he replied. It was one of his little jokes, said with a faint smile that left sharp little barbs just beneath her skin.

In the past she would have felt the need to defend her choice to take her first vacation in such a long time. She might even have added that she had spent the first week of that vacation dealing personally with the very client he had mentioned. She might have reminded him that she had returned to work nearly a week sooner than she had planned, still limping on a swollen ankle.

She wouldn't, of course, have added that she had gone back to the office only because she couldn't stand to spend a full day moping around her empty apartment and thinking about Gideon.

"Good point, Dad," was all she said instead. "The fruit is really good this morning, isn't it?"

"I wish Adrienne was here," Isabelle lamented, over Lenore's Sunday lunch of fried chicken, creamed potatoes and white gravy, fried okra, corn on the cob and tender turnip greens.

It was one of Gideon's favorite meals, but Isabelle's artless comment made his appetite evaporate.

"Have you heard from Adrienne since she went back to New York?" Caitlin asked from the other side of the table.

"Of course I've heard from her, she's my agent." They had spoken exactly twice during the past three weeks—for a total of perhaps twenty minutes. Adrienne had used exactly the same tone with him that she had before her visit—briskly, professionally impersonal.

Both calls had left him feeling irritable, restless and empty, pacing his house for hours before sitting down to stare fruitlessly at his computer.

He wasn't sleeping, wasn't eating well, wasn't satisfied with his writing—and he didn't know what the hell to do about it.

"I miss her," Isabelle said.

Gideon sighed. "Yeah, kiddo. So do I."

Eyeing his brother with speculation, Nathan changed the subject, for which Gideon would be eternally grateful.

From her office window, Adrienne could see more office windows. Hundreds of them, filled with other people going about the business of making a living. She wondered how many of them loved their work. How many of them would go home this evening to a family who loved them or a personal life that fulfilled them.

"Adrienne," Jacqueline bustled into the room with a stack of outgoing correspondence in one hand and a bundle of incoming mail in the other. "Giselle Eastwood is on line two. She's hysterical again, just wants you to sweet-talk her for a few minutes and assure her how wonderful she is. I told her you're terribly busy, but she insisted that I tell you she's on the phone."

Adrienne groaned. "I just spent an hour last week stroking her ego. She needs another fix already?"

"Apparently, she's had another argument with her editor over revisions. You know how she gets when anyone suggests changing her work.''

That remark, of course, made her think about Gideon. She was doing better, actually. It had been at least ten minutes since the last time she'd thought about him.

''Adrienne? What do I do about Giselle?''

Recalled to her present surroundings, Adrienne blinked. ''Oh. I'll take the call, I guess. I'll give her a quick pep talk and then you can buzz me so I'll have an excuse to disconnect.''

''That won't be a problem. I'm sure you'll have a half dozen more calls come in by the time I get back to my desk.''

''Tell me something I don't know.'' Sometimes Adrienne felt as though the telephone was going to attach itself permanently to the side of her head. She could certainly understand why Gideon had formed such an abhorrence for the instrument.

And there she went, thinking about him again. With a sigh and a shake of her head, she picked up the receiver. ''Good morning, Giselle. What can I do for you today?''

Gideon stared out his office window and watched lightning streak across the midnight sky, creating an eerie strobe-light effect of the woods spread around him. Rain pounded against the roof above him and streamed down the panes of the window glass.

Yet behind him there was silence and utter stillness, as if he stood in a solitary bubble within the storm. He could almost fancy himself a prisoner there, the doors and windows guarded by the ferocious force of the hovering thunderstorm.

Stupid, he thought in sudden self-disgust, turning abruptly away from the window. Pushing a hand through his shaggy hair, he reminded himself that he was no male Rapunzel and there was no Princess Charming battling the elements to rescue him from his loneliness.

Exactly the way he wanted it. He had, after all, chosen to live this way. Fairy tales fell apart when examined too closely, and dashing heroes—and heroines—all too often proved to have feet of clay.

He would prefer to think of the storm as answerable to him—not holding him here but keeping away those who would disturb him, shatter his valued tranquillity or threaten the contentment he'd found in his sanctuary.

It was a measure of his pensive mood that he was personifying the storm in the first place. He'd always been fanciful—he was a writer, after all—but it seemed that lately he'd been drifting more and more into his imagination. Pulling farther away from the rest of the world. As often as he assured himself he wanted nothing more, his isolation was beginning to worry him.

Did he really want to spend the rest of his life this way? Was it already too late to change his course, even if he decided he wanted to try?

Adrienne was having a really lousy day. It seemed as though it had been one battle after another, from tracing a missing royalty check for one client to fighting for a bigger advance for another. There was a rather terse parting of ways with another author, who blamed Adrienne for his floundering career, even though she had advised him several times that he'd been headed for trouble.

By two in the afternoon she had a headache that seemed to spread all the way down into her shoulders.

"Someday," she muttered, rubbing her aching temples, "I really am going to quit this job."

"You might want to wait until tomorrow," Jacqueline

said from the open doorway. Her dark eyes were a bit wider than usual, and she had a hand resting on her heart as if to signify its pounding. "There is the most delicious man waiting out there to see you."

Adrienne frowned and glanced at her calendar. "I don't have an appointment scheduled, do I?"

"No, but I think you'll want to work him in. The man is gorgeous—green eyes, dark hair, a face that should be on a billboard. Body to die for. All male, if you know what I mean—no having to ask yourself if this one is straight. And he's got a sexy Southern drawl that I could listen to all afternoon."

Her own heart was pounding now. "Gideon is here?"

Jacqueline chuckled. "Didn't have any trouble recognizing the description, did you?"

"Oh, my God." With an instinct as old as woman, she raised both hands to smooth her hair.

"Want me to tell him you're too busy to see him?"

Adrienne gave her grinning assistant a look. "I'll see him."

"I thought you might."

Standing behind her desk, she was still trying to decide how to greet him—a smile, a handshake, an air kiss near his cheek?—when he entered her office. Looking as delectable as Jacqueline had described, in khakis and a forest-green shirt, he stopped on the other side of her desk and tossed a thick manila envelope in front of her. "I sent this directly to my editor, but I thought you might want a copy."

"You finished your book."

"Yeah."

She moistened her lips. "So you just decided to…bring me a copy?"

"You know how I am about telephones."

"I can't believe you're here."

He glanced at the window, through which they could see all those other buildings. "I'm finding that a bit hard to believe, myself."

An awkward silence fell for a moment between them, and then Gideon said, "You look good, Adrienne."

"So do you."

"When can you get out of here?"

"Now."

His eyebrows rose. "You don't have a full calendar for the afternoon?"

"Not anymore." She picked up her purse and the envelope he'd brought her, leaving everything else where it lay.

His rare smile flashed, and he crooked his arm to her. "Let's go."

Electricity surged through her when she laid her fingers on his arm. Their eyes met, and she smiled, her skin feeling warm and tingly beneath her clothing.

They had almost made it out of the office when her father stepped into the doorway, blocking their way. Peering at them over his half glasses, he raised his eyebrows. "What's this?"

Adrienne dropped her hand from Gideon's arm. "Gideon McCloud, this is my father, Lawrence Corley."

Gideon raked the older man with a cool glance. "Nice to meet you," he said, though his tone belied the words.

Lawrence wore the smile he reserved for valued business associates. "It's a pleasure to meet you, Mr. McCloud. I'm a great admirer of your work."

Mostly because that work had brought in a generous fifteen percent, Adrienne added in cynical silence.

"Thanks. I attribute much of my success, of course, to

my agent. She's one of the most dedicated professionals I've ever dealt with."

"Thank you. I've trained her in the business from the time she was just a teenager."

And he took full credit for everything she had become, Adrienne thought in resignation—despite her formal education and the years of hard work she had spent learning the business.

"You didn't tell me you were expecting Mr. McCloud this afternoon, Adrienne."

"She didn't know. I dropped in without calling first."

"I see." Lawrence's expressive silver eyebrows rose again. "Then you were fortunate to find her in. We all have very tight schedules around here, you know."

"I can imagine. Now, if you'll excuse me, we were just on our way out."

Adrienne rather enjoyed seeing her father caught off balance, if only for a moment. "You're leaving?"

"Yes." Adrienne met his eyes, challenging him to protest.

"You, um, don't have anything pending?"

"Jacqueline can take care of everything for me."

"But I needed to speak to you about—"

"It can wait." It was one of the first times in her life Adrienne had interrupted her father. It felt pretty good, actually.

Lawrence was much too professional to show his displeasure in front of a client, but she knew he would express himself later, when they were alone. "When will you be back?"

Gideon put his hands on her shoulders and guided her toward the doorway. "We'll let you know."

It was probably the first time Lawrence had heard his daughter giggle since she was a teenager. She didn't look around to see how he reacted. At that moment she only had eyes for Gideon McCloud.

"I like your apartment."

"How would you know? You haven't actually seen any of it."

His weight propped on an elbow as he loomed over her in her bed, he grinned. "Okay, then, I like your bedroom."

"Thank you." They had barely made it through the front door before he'd swung her into his arms and carried her to bed. They hadn't discussed their intentions after leaving her office, but had, instead, come straight to her apartment by mutual unspoken agreement.

"I've missed you," she said, rubbing her hand down his firm, bare arm.

"I missed you, too."

It rather surprised her that he had admitted it, even though he wouldn't have come if he hadn't missed her. "I still can't believe you're here."

He slid his fingertips along her jawline. "You keep saying that."

"I know. I can't help it. I simply never expected you to walk into my office today."

"It was sort of an impulse. I finished the book, and the next thing I knew I was reserving a seat on an airline. I walked into your office half expecting you to look horrified to see me."

She laughed and rubbed her cheek against his hand. "I'm sure you could tell I was delighted to see you."

"Actually, yeah, I could. And it was quite a relief."

"Did you really miss me?"

"What do you want, Adrienne, flowery phrases?"

His indulgent tone made her smile. "Yes."

"I missed you very much."

She laughed and tugged him down on top of her. "Well, it's not exactly poetry. But it means a great deal more to me," she added.

He kissed her lingeringly. "I'm pretty mad at you, actually," he murmured when he raised his head.

If this was mad, she wasn't complaining, just a bit curious. "Why?"

"I had no intention of following you here. I was going to be perfectly content to go back to the way things were before you showed up on my doorstep."

She nibbled at his lower lip. "I messed things up, hmm?"

"You could say that. You made me want…more."

She wasn't sure what he meant by "more"—or if he even knew at this point. As he covered her mouth with his, she decided to just be glad that he was here now.

It was hunger that finally drove them out of the bed. Dressed in a short, red satin robe, Adrienne made chicken salad sandwiches, which she served with baked chips and some leftover fruit salad.

"How long can you stay?" she asked as they ate at the chrome-and-glass table in her airy, modern kitchen.

He swallowed a sip of iced Chai tea. "I'm not on any particular schedule. Thought I might stay through the weekend if that's not inconvenient for you."

"Not at all. You'll stay here, of course."

"I was hoping you would ask."

She nodded, mentally rearranging schedules and making lists of nonessential appointments she could cancel during his stay. "How's Isabelle?"

She watched as his face softened a bit. "She's fine. I spent an hour at the park with her yesterday afternoon. She wanted me to tell you hello. She said she'd have sent you a drawing if I'd given her more notice that I was coming.''

Pleased that he was still making an effort to stay in contact with his little sister, she smiled. ''I have her other drawing hanging in my office.''

''I know. I saw it. She'll be tickled when I tell her.''

''Have you ever been to New York before?''

''Other than to change planes on my way to London a few years ago, I haven't.''

''Is there anything in particular you would like to see or do while you're here?''

He shrugged. ''I'm not here as a tourist. I came to see you.''

She laughed. ''Do you suppose other people actually plan visits with each other—with advance notice and reservations and other minor details like that?''

His eyes gleamed with shared amusement. ''No one I know.''

''I'll have to go to the office for a few hours in the morning, and I have a meeting Saturday afternoon I can't really get out of, but I should be free most of the weekend.''

''Take care of your business. I'm perfectly capable of entertaining myself while you're occupied.''

And then what? Did he see this only as a brief visit—a reward to himself for finishing the book? A little rest, a little sex, a little fun before diving into the next project?

Was he envisioning more encounters like this in their future? Brief visits a couple of times a year, perhaps, until one or the other tired of them and moved on?

A no-strings, nonexclusive, long-distance affair. Was that what he had in mind? She found the prospect depressing, but she wasn't quite ready to explore his thoughts just yet. ''Would you like some more tea?''

"Yeah," he said. "Thanks."

Live in the moment, she reminded herself. It wouldn't serve any purpose to fret about a future she had no way of predicting.

Late Saturday afternoon Gideon let himself into Adrienne's apartment with the key she had left him. He paused for a moment to study her trendy decor, trying to decide if he liked it. It wasn't bad, he concluded finally. Just not…homey. It reminded him more of the Manhattan art galleries he had visited than of someone's living room. He had a hard time imagining himself propping his feet on her chrome-and-glass coffee table and watching football on her TV—even if she had one in here.

Wandering into the kitchen, he made coffee in her space-age coffeemaker. He'd spent the afternoon the same way he had entertained himself yesterday morning while she'd cleared away pressing business at the office. He'd done the tourist thing, roaming the streets of Manhattan by cab and foot, studying the sights and the people, soaking in the atmosphere. Trying to imagine himself living here.

After all, he'd told himself, a writer could work anywhere—and there were damn sure plenty of them who called this crowded island home. What did it really matter where he lived as long as he had his computer, his ideas—and Adrienne? He was the mobile one. It would be stupid to expect her to give up her life here and move back to Mississippi with him.

As if she would even consider doing so.

Restless, he paced through her apartment, trying not to leave footprints on her plush, steel-gray carpet. Like him she had turned an extra bedroom into a home office, hers furnished with matching steel-and-laminate office furniture, unlike his own haphazard mix of woods.

Also unlike his own work space, hers was immaculate, the surfaces uncluttered. The only thing on her desk was a large manila envelope that looked ominously familiar. He saw Dylan's name on the outside of the package when he moved closer, and he realized it was the one that had caused the quarrel between Adrienne and him the day she had left Honesty. The envelope looked a bit more battered than it had the last time he'd seen it; it had obviously been opened and the contents removed more than once.

He had deliberately not asked Adrienne about Dylan—whether she had spoken with him since she'd left Honesty, whether he really had written a book and, if so, whether it was any good. He'd only seen Dylan once in passing since that day in his kitchen, and they had greeted each other only with cool looks.

What twist of fate had brought Dylan back into his life at this stage through Adrienne? The fact that he'd been there to assist her after the rental-car accident, that he and Adrienne had become so friendly and that Dylan had been secretly planning to follow in Gideon's writing footsteps, how could Gideon have predicted any of those things?

He didn't even want to think of how Deborah would have reacted if she had walked into that cozy impromptu party in Gideon's kitchen on that Sunday afternoon.

He studied the unsealed envelope with a scowl. He would hate it, of course, if anyone walked into his office and read something without his permission. He didn't like anyone messing with his stuff.

This situation was even more problematic because it involved both Adrienne's privacy and Dylan Smith's. Not that he particularly cared about the latter, of course. And he *had* opened his own office completely to Adrienne, giving her free access to everything in there.

''Ah, hell,'' he muttered, snatching up the envelope. ''They can sue me.''

Chapter Fifteen

The meeting lasted longer than Adrienne had planned. Though she knew Gideon didn't expect her to entertain him, she was still in a hurry to get back to him. Mostly because she didn't want to waste any of her time with him.

It had been a very nice visit so far. They had been totally absorbed in each other, carefully avoiding any sensitive subjects. They had not talked about the future or their pasts or their families, yet there had been few awkward silences between them. And on a physical level, well, they had no trouble at all communicating in that respect.

She didn't even want to think about how badly she was going to miss him when he left.

He was sitting on the Italian leather sofa in her living room when she walked in. His expression was so grim that she stumbled a little. "What's wrong?"

He nodded toward a stack of papers on her coffee table. "I rifled through your things today."

Confused, she took a step forward. "I don't mind—oh."

Recognizing the pages, she looked back up at him. "You read Dylan's book?"

"Most of it."

She set her things down and moved toward him. "You know he wouldn't have wanted you to read it without his permission."

"I imagine he would absolutely hate that I did it."

She frowned at him. "I never thought you would go through my papers."

"You have every right to be angry with me."

"Oh, I am," she replied, and she was, she assured herself. Not furious, but highly annoyed.

"I won't do it again. Wouldn't have this time if I hadn't seen Smith's name on it. I'm not exactly rational when it comes to that guy, you know."

It was said in a rueful tone that failed to make her smile. "I'm aware of that."

She sat in an armchair and crossed her arms over her chest. "Well? Since you read it, what did you think of it?"

His dark scowl gave her the answer. If he had hated Dylan's book, he would be smiling. "You liked it," she said.

"It's okay," he muttered, barely loud enough for her to hear him.

"It's better than okay. It's a very good first book. With just a little polishing, there's no reason at all why it shouldn't be published. I think he has the beginning of a potentially successful mystery series."

"Yes, so do I." Gideon looked even more disgruntled as he made the admission. "You're going to represent him."

It wasn't a question, but she waited a beat before replying. "No. I've spent the past couple of weeks making some notes for suggested revisions he might want to consider before sending it out again. I'm also sending him a list of reputable agents that I think might be interested in his work."

She'd certainly gotten Gideon's attention. He sat up straight on the couch and stared at her. "Why would you do that? We just agreed, the book's good."

"Yes, and normally I would be pleased to work with him. But in this case there seems to be a conflict of interest."

"Me."

She merely inclined her head. It had taken her nearly three weeks of internal debate before she had finally accepted that she couldn't represent both Gideon and Dylan without eventually encountering problems because of it.

Gideon's scowl had deepened. "You're really turning him down?"

"You asked me to," she reminded him.

He glowered at her a moment, then firmly shook his head. "You aren't pushing this off on me. Dylan will tell everyone you turned him down because I was threatened by him. You've got to take him."

"You're the one who said you didn't want me to represent Dylan," she repeated.

"That was before I knew he was any good."

"Gideon, you make me crazy." She shook her head in exasperation. "You don't really know what you want, do you?"

"I want *you.*" He was on his feet now, a look in his eyes that she knew very well. "And I owe you an apology for invading your privacy."

She placed her hands in his outstretched palms and allowed him to draw her to her feet, but she couldn't help pointing out, "We haven't really resolved anything, you know."

"Sure we have. I've agreed to stay out of your personal papers and your business."

He probably thought she would be pleased by that promise, but instead she found it rather depressing. It sounded so…detached. Neatly separating and compartmentalizing their lives.

He pulled her close against him when he kissed her, and she tried to find solace in the unmistakable evidence of his desire for her. She had never expected forever from him, she reminded herself as his mouth moved enticingly against hers. Even these few days together were more than she had expected when she'd left him in Mississippi five weeks ago.

She supposed she should be relieved that he wasn't going to protest her representing Dylan, if she decided to do so. It was a very mature and professional concession, coming from Gideon.

So why did it feel as though they were moving even further apart?

Gideon woke in the middle of the night and found himself alone in Adrienne's bed. It was a startling experience, because he was usually such a light sleeper that any noise or movement woke him. He must have been more tired than he'd realized.

Because he knew he wouldn't sleep again until he'd made sure Adrienne was okay, he slipped out of the sheets and stepped into the jeans he'd left lying beside the bed. Following a faint trail of light, he padded silently into the living room, where he found Adrienne.

She sat in a chair with her bare feet curled beneath her. The only light in the room came from the lamp beside her.

It gleamed in her auburn hair, glowed in the ruby satin of her short robe and glittered off the tears sliding slowly down her cheeks.

He took a quick step forward. "Adrienne?"

A sudden, bright smile belied her tears. "You changed the ending."

Only then did he see the stack of papers lying in her lap. "My book?" he hazarded.

Setting the manuscript on the table beside her, she leaped to her feet, crossed to him and slid her arms around his waist, resting her cheek against his bare chest. "It's wonderful. I love it."

His arms closed automatically around her. His cheek found a natural resting place against her soft, lush hair. "I'm glad you liked it."

"When did you decide to bring Alanya back to life?"

"A couple of weeks after you left, when I finally acknowledged that you were right. I was just being stubborn when I refused to consider your suggestions."

She beamed up at him. "I thought it would be a good idea, but you were the one who made it work so beautifully. That was one of the most emotionally rewarding endings I've ever read."

"You," he told her with a slight lump in his throat, "are hardly objective."

"Being crazy about you doesn't affect my judgment about your writing," she informed him loftily.

The lump grew until it almost choked him. When she said she was crazy about him, what did she mean, exactly? Was it only a figure of speech? An offhanded expression of casual affection? Or was it more?

Maybe he was the one who was just plain crazy.

"I'm glad you like it," he repeated, because he couldn't think of anything else to say.

She rose on tiptoe to press a kiss against his lips. "You have real talent with a love scene, Gideon McCloud."

A surge of heat went through him. "You could say I've found a great source of inspiration."

Her throaty chuckle was lost in the depths of his plundering kiss.

Having showered, applied her makeup and dressed in a comfortable peasant top and drawstring linen pants, Adrienne exited her bathroom Sunday morning prepared to spend a nice, leisurely day with Gideon.

She hadn't expected to find him packing his suitcase, looking as though he were getting ready to leave. "What are you doing?"

He looked at her with an expression that made her chest clench. "It isn't going to work, Adrienne."

Her hand wasn't quite steady when she set down the hairbrush she had been carrying on the dresser. "What isn't going to work?"

He motioned vaguely toward the window. "I thought I could make my own place here, figure out a way to create my own space where I wouldn't have to deal with people. In some ways, I thought I could find even more privacy in a big city where no one knows me or my family or our business. Instead I just feel smothered by the sheer numbers of people here. It's as if I can almost feel them pressing against the walls and windows of this apartment."

It was his vivid imagination that made him such a wonderful writer, of course. And it was his reluctant attachment to the charming little town where he had grown up that made him so intriguing.

But it was his sheer arrogance that made him the most exasperating man she had ever met.

"So you're leaving."

He zipped his bag. "I can change a story's ending for you, but I can't change who I am. I couldn't do it for my family and, I'm sorry, but I can't do it for you, either."

She locked her arms over her chest, one foot beginning to tap against the carpet. "Funny. I don't remember asking you to change anything but the ending to your story. And, if you'll remember, even that suggestion was in response to your request for my input."

He sighed. "Look, I'm not trying to blame you for anything. I'm the one who had to find out if I could make this work. And if it makes you feel any better, you're the only woman I've ever considered changing for."

"I suppose I should be flattered."

He searched her face with a frown. "You're angry."

"That's an understatement," she replied through clenched teeth.

"Because I'm leaving?"

"Actually, that sounds like a very good idea right now."

Because she really needed coffee, she turned to leave the bedroom. His hand on her arm spun her around again.

"I never said I could stay," he reminded her.

"I never asked you to stay," she snapped back. "Now let go of my arm."

Instead of releasing her, he held on, looking even more confused. "So you're angry because I considered staying? Because you didn't *want* anything permanent to develop between us?"

"How can such a brilliant writer be such a stupid man?" She tugged at her arm. "Let me go."

"Just wait a minute, will you? I'm trying to figure out what you're so mad about. Is it because I'm leaving or because I thought about staying?"

"It's because you're so arrogant that you never even discussed the possibility of staying with me! And because you're either so selfish or so cowardly that you refuse to share any part of yourself with me—or with anyone else who cares about you, for that matter.''

Now he was the one who was angry, his emerald eyes flashing with temper. ''That's garbage.''

''You pride yourself on being such a self-contained loner, and you act like you're doing everyone else such a favor when you let them into your life for a little while. You pretend you don't really need anyone, rather than admitting how lucky you are to have such a nice family, who have been much too patient and indulgent with you, in my opinion.''

He had finally released her arm. ''You don't know what you're talking about.''

''Don't I? You claim New York is too crowded for you, when the truth is that you simply like living in Honesty. You like the people there, even though you treat them so shabbily, and you don't want to live so far away from them or from the family you ignore so shamelessly. So you've been hurt a few times, well, who hasn't? What gives you the right to treat other people this way just because you're afraid of being hurt again?''

''I am not a coward.''

She was angry and hurt enough to be reckless. ''Really? Have you read your father's letter yet?''

His eyes narrowed to furious slits. ''My father has nothing to do with this.''

''Doesn't he? What about his second wife? Isabelle's mother? Your girlfriend, I understand.''

''Who told you that?''

She didn't recoil from the sharpness of his question, but it took an effort to hold her ground. ''Not you, obviously. You didn't let me into your life that much, but you thought about moving here to grace me with your company for a little while. And then you accused me of trying to change you, just like your father did. Well, I never asked you for anything, including clarifications of some of the rumors I heard while I was in your hometown, and I damn well resent being lumped with everyone in your past who let you down.''

"Let me make something clear—Kimberly was never my girlfriend. I dated her a few times, casually, before she got involved with my father's campaign and my father. I wasn't seeing her at the time she started dating him, hadn't been interested in seeing her for several months, and the only reason I cared that he was sleeping with her was because his selfish behavior was so devastating for my mother and my sister. I've never held any of those circumstances against Isabelle, and I haven't carried a torch for her mother. Is there any other gossip about my past you'd like to discuss?''

She wasn't angry now. Just sad. "Don't you see, Gideon? I didn't want to force you to tell me those things. If you expected me to be an important part of your life, you should have wanted to share your thoughts and your feelings with me. You should have been willing to take a few emotional risks.''

"What would you have said if I had taken a risk and asked you to move back to Honesty with me?'' he challenged her.

Though her heart clenched, she lifted her chin defiantly, knowing he still didn't fully comprehend what she had said. "You'll never know, will you? You were too stubborn to ask.''

He hesitated long enough to make her wonder if he was going to ask now, but then he turned and picked up his bag. "I'll get a cab to the airport," he said. "I'm sorry everything turned out this way. I hope it won't interfere with our working relationship.''

She might have laughed at that, if she could have found even a trace of bitter humor inside her. ''I don't see why it should. I'll take a lesson from you and lock my personal feelings inside where no one else can see them or examine them too closely. It seems to work so well for you.''

''Adrienne—''

''I'll have my assistant give you a call next week about those contracts you need to sign. We'll express them to you so we can get the next project underway without much delay. Your publisher will be in contact with you about the details of the promotional events you've agreed to. If there's anything else I can do for you, feel free to send me an e-mail or give Jacqueline a call.''

He didn't seem to know how to respond to her brusquely professional tone. On one hand, it must have been a relief to him that they were no longer treading on dangerous emotional ground, but the way he was looking at her told her that he hated leaving this way.

Maybe it was best that it had happened like this. Clean and final. She wouldn't be left wondering when he might show up on her doorstep again, waiting for calls that might never come, hoping for something that would never happen. They should never have confused their business relationship with a physical element, and she should never have let her heart get involved when she'd known all along that he kept his own locked tightly away.

''I'll call you,'' he said finally.

She did laugh then, a sound that was painful even to her. ''I wonder how many women you've said that to as you walked away. And I wonder how many of them were foolish enough to believe it.''

Muttering something she couldn't hear—and didn't try

to—he turned and left the room, his shoulders stiff, his bag gripped in a white-knuckled fist.

She had no doubt that he was hurting a bit. After all, he'd cared enough to think about moving here, she reminded herself as she sank numbly to the edge of her still-tumbled bed. But he would get over it. He had so much more practice than she did at creating a safe new world for himself.

Adrienne wasn't in a good mood on Monday morning. She snapped at her father, was impatient with her assistant, snarled at an editor. When she realized what she was doing, she made herself take a deep breath and force a smile onto her face. It wasn't fair of her to take out her pain and anger on other people, she reminded herself.

That was the sort of thing Gideon McCloud would do.

And so she looked around with forced patience when a sound from her office doorway distracted her from a difficult letter she was trying to write. "What can I do for you, Ja—"

She fell silent when she saw the man standing in her doorway.

"Don't blame your assistant for not announcing me," Gideon said, closing the door behind him. "I sort of barged past her."

She wanted to rise, but she wasn't sure her legs would support her. "I thought you'd gone back to Mississippi."

"No." He set his bag on the floor at his feet. "I spent the night in a hotel. I decided during the night that there's something I need to do before I leave."

She cleared her throat. "What?"

"Ask you to go with me."

It was a good thing she was sitting down, she decided.

She would surely have fallen if she hadn't been. "You—"

He took a step toward the desk, his expression grimly determined. "You're right, you know. I was afraid to ask—still am, I guess. It's going to hurt like hell if you say no. Not to mention being a rather humiliating experience. It's the sort of risk I've been careful to avoid my entire adult life."

"Then why—"

"Because you've changed me," he answered before she could even complete the question. "You didn't ask me to change, but I changed, anyway. I know now that my house is never going to feel like a home again without you in it. And I know that if you can't see yourself living there with me, then I'll have to figure out a way to live here with you, if you'll have me."

She finally found the strength to rise, but she didn't move toward him. "You just suddenly decided all of this?"

"I can understand why you'd be skeptical, considering the things I said to you yesterday," he acknowledged. "But it isn't as impulsive as it seems. I was already thinking along these lines when I came to New York. And then yesterday, well, I guess I panicked. I didn't want to admit that I was the coward you accused me of being, so I sort of blamed everything on you."

"You panicked," she repeated.

He shrugged sheepishly. "I've never asked a woman to marry me before. It was a knee-jerk reaction to get cold feet at the last minute and try to run."

"Marry." She fell into her chair again when her knees folded. She'd known the feelings between them were strong—strong enough to draw him away from his home, strong enough to frighten him into running again—but she had never expected this. "You're asking me to marry you?"

"I guess I am."

"Why?"

"The usual reasons." He cleared his throat. "I've been in love with you since the night you walked into my house and found Isabelle's owl. I knew it almost immediately, but I fought it. Thought I would get over it. Now I know that I won't."

She locked her fingers in her lap, forcing her eyes to stay dry, her voice even. "It isn't the most poetic proposal any woman has ever received."

"No," he said with a grimace. "But it's an honest one."

One more time she pushed herself to her feet. "I'd much rather have honesty than poetry."

"So would I." He moved another step toward her. "You don't have to give me an answer now. I realize we've only known each other a few weeks—other than the strictly professional relationship we've had for the past couple of years, of course. I just thought you should know that I—"

"The answer is yes," she said gently. "We'll have to do some compromising about where we'll live—maybe we can keep a home in Honesty and an apartment here for business purposes. But those details don't matter right now as much as the fact that you love me and that you trust me enough to tell me so."

He looked as though he wasn't sure he'd heard her correctly. "You're saying yes?"

She smiled mistily at his hesitation. "Yes. I love you, too, Gideon."

Fast? Yes. But maybe she had been in love with him before she'd ever even met him. Maybe she had fallen in love with a voice on the telephone or with the man who had written the books that had spoken so deeply to her.

All she knew for certain was that she had gone to Mississippi and had found the home she hadn't even realized she was looking for.

He swallowed hard. "So you're saying you will marry me."

Suddenly she couldn't stop smiling. "Did you think I was going to say no? Are you sorry now that you asked?"

His own smile was a bit shaky. "No. Just scared to my toenails."

That little slice of honesty affected her almost more than anything else he'd said yet. It told her exactly how hard it had been for him to reach out to her. Just how difficult it was for him to change the safe, solitary life he'd created for himself. And exactly how much he loved her, that he was willing to do so despite the fear.

She moved around the desk and put her arms around his neck. "You'd better not change your mind, Gideon McCloud, because I plan to have you sign a contract for life."

"That contract binds both ways, you know," he reminded her as his arms closed around her.

She lifted her mouth to his to seal the deal.

Epilogue

"**Y**our father looked kind of shell-shocked during the wedding," Gideon mused a month later as he poured champagne into two crystal flutes. "Do you think he really believed you would change your mind at the last minute?"

She laughed as she accepted one of the flutes and sank to the side of the hotel bed with it. She still wore the tailored white suit she had worn for their simple but absolutely beautiful wedding, though she'd kicked off the toe-cramping white heels. "As much as I hate to defend him, we can't really blame him for feeling as though his head is spinning. In only four weeks I've announced my engagement, restructured my entire career, moved to Mississippi and gotten married. Even your family is still having a little trouble processing the changes."

"My family is stunned but delighted," he assured her, sitting beside her. The light from the bedside lamp glittered off the plain gold ring on his left hand.

"To family—" she said, holding up her glass with a smile "—problems and all."

"Speaking of which—" Setting his flute on the night-stand, Gideon reached into his suit coat and removed something from the inside pocket. "I thought you'd want to know that I read this today."

She glanced at the folded sheet of paper, then felt her eyes widen. "Is that...?"

"My father's letter. I thought I should finally read it, so you can stop fretting about it. Today seemed like a good time, since nothing he could have said would have put me in a bad mood."

She searched his face, finding nothing but a calm contentment there. "Was there anything important in it?"

"It must have been written just before he left for the vacation in which he had his fatal accident. He said he was sorry that he and I had never been able to resolve our differences. He had just finished reading my latest book, and he thought he should tell me that he had read and enjoyed all of them. He thought I would be very successful as a writer, especially if I would take his advice about a few things he saw as weaknesses in my style."

She winced. "At least he was trying to reach out to you."

"He was trying to take charge of my writing career, since he finally realized I was going to make a go of it. As far as he was concerned, he had given me enough time to get over being mad at him for betraying Mom, and it was time for him to get involved in my life again."

"How did that make you feel?"

He shrugged. "Annoyed that he never understood exactly how much he hurt the family with his actions. Incredulous that he thought we all just needed a little time to get over it and accept what he'd done. And..."

"And?" she urged when he paused as if in search of words.

"Maybe a little pleased that he read the books," he admitted finally. "I never knew whether he'd read them or not. I guess it shouldn't matter to me that he did, but…"

"But he was your father, and it does matter, no matter how many times he let you down," she concluded. "Trust me, I understand."

"I guess you do." He wrapped an arm around her and pulled her against him. "No one has ever understood me better than you do. No one ever will."

She laid her head on her husband's shoulder. "I love you, Gideon."

"I love you, too."

It was getting easier for him to say it, she thought in satisfaction, lifting her mouth to his.

It would get even easier with a lifetime of practice.

*   *   *   *   *

Look for the story of
Deborah McCloud and Dylan Smith in

FAITH, HOPE AND FAMILY (SE 1538),

the next book in Gina Wilkins's
THE McCLOUDS OF MISSISSIPPI
miniseries, only from
Silhouette Special Edition.
On sale May 2003
For a sneak preview turn the page…

Chapter One

The Honesty city limits sign was just visible within the range of Deborah McCloud's headlights. She was tempted to keep driving, leaving her home town behind her. Honesty, Mississippi, wasn't her home anymore—she'd escaped nine years ago when she left for college, and she hadn't been back home for more than a few days at a time. It was only because her mother and two older brothers still lived here that she returned at all.

It might have been a Freudian impulse that made her press harder on the accelerator as she moved closer to the edge of town. Probably a barely suppressed desire to escape the unhappy memories here, though she tried not to dwell on them during her infrequent visits with her mother. She supposed it was her brother's wedding that afternoon that had brought the memories so close to the surface tonight, preventing her from sleeping.

A flash of blue lights in her rearview mirror made her

hiss a curse between her teeth. *Terrific,* she thought, pulling over to the side of the deserted road. The only thing that would make this episode worse was if the officer who had pulled her over was Dylan Smith. Surely fate wouldn't be so cruel.

She should have known better.

Resting one hand on the top of her car, Dylan studied her through the open driver's door window. Even though he was silhouetted by the yellowish streetlamps above him, she had no trouble picturing his roughly handsome face, nor his bitingly intense steel-gray eyes. The dark brown hair he had once worn rebel-long was now cut almost militarily short, befitting his career on the right side of the law.

When he spoke, his voice was deeper than the youthful echo that still too frequently haunted her dreams, but held the familiar mocking undercurrent of humor. "'Evening, Ms. McCloud. Did you rob a bank? Knock over a liquor store? You seem to be in a big hurry to get out of town."

Knowing her own face was illuminated by the same light that shadowed his, she kept her expression impassive. "I'm not leaving town. I just felt like taking a drive."

"At midnight?"

"Yes. Is that against the law?"

If her challenging tone annoyed him, he didn't let it show. "No. But doing 65 in a 45-mile-an-hour zone is."

"So write me a ticket." She extracted her drivers license from her wallet and held it out to him. "If you run this, you'll see that I have no outstanding warrants."

He made no move to take the drivers license. "You know I'm not going to ticket you."

"You'd ticket any other speeder. I expect the same treatment."

Leaving his hands where they were, he asked, "How was your brother's wedding?"

The abrupt change of subject made her blink. She lowered her outstretched hand to her lap. "It was fine. No problems."

"That's nice. Gideon and Adrienne make a great couple."

"Yes, they do." Keeping her voice totally disinterested, she said, "I heard that Adrienne insisted on inviting you. How come you didn't show up?"

"It's not like you to ask stupid questions."

His curt reply made her temper flare again. "Then I'm sorry I asked."

He sighed. "I didn't want any unpleasantness to cast a shadow over the wedding. I knew you wouldn't want me there. And, despite my new friendship with Adrienne, Gideon and I still barely speak. For their sake, and for your mother's, I didn't want to risk any problems."

"I really couldn't care less if you were there or not. And my mother would have been as gracious to you as she was to any of the other guests."

He obviously didn't buy her implication that he no longer had the power to stir her emotions, even negative ones, but he didn't challenge her on that. "I always admired your mother, you know. A real class act. The way she'd being so kind to her ex-husband's orphaned little girl, well, that just confirms what I always thought about her."

Deborah had no intention of discussing her family scandals with him. "I'm sure my mother would be pleased that you think so highly of her."

He made a sound that might have been a laugh. "I'm sure your mother couldn't care less what I think of her."

She tapped the steering wheel again. ''Are you going to write me a ticket or not?''

This time his laugh was a bit more natural. The one that had always warmed some cold spot deep inside her heart— and would do so again now if she hadn't steeled herself against it. ''I don't think I've ever had a speeder actually demand a citation from me before.''

She scowled. ''Well?''

''No ticket. I'll just advise you to slow down for the remainder of your drive.''

''Then I'm free to go?''

He dropped his arms to his side and stepped back from the car. His voice was suddenly weary when he replied, ''I've never tried to stop you from leaving, Deborah.''

Not trusting herself to speak, she put the car in gear and drove away, well aware that he remained where he was until she was out of his sight.

*   *   *   *   *

Secrets and passion abound
as the royals reclaim their throne!

Bestselling author

RAYE MORGAN

brings you a special installment
of her new miniseries

ROYAL NIGHTS

On sale May 2003

When a terrifying act of sabotage nearly takes the life of Prince Damian
of Nabotavia, he is plunged into a world of darkness. Hell-bent on
discovering who tried to kill him, the battle-scarred prince searches
tirelessly for the truth. The unwavering support of Sara, his fearless
therapist, is the only light in Damian's bleak world. But will revealing
his most closely guarded secret throw Sara into the line of fire?

Don't miss the other books in this exciting miniseries:

JACK AND THE PRINCESS (Silhouette Romance #1655)
On sale April 2003

BETROTHED TO THE PRINCE (Silhouette Romance #1667)
On sale June 2003

COUNTERFEIT PRINCESS (Silhouette Romance #1672)
On sale July 2003

Available wherever Silhouette books are sold.

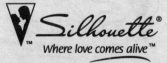

Where love comes alive™

Visit Silhouette at www.eHarlequin.com   PSRN

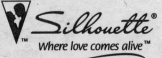

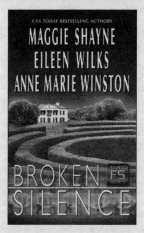

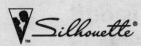

COMING NEXT MONTH

SSECNM0403